NO CASTLES HERE

NO CASTLES HERE

A.C.E. BAUER

RANDOM HOUSE · NEW YORK

Published in the United States by Random House Children's Books,
a division of Random House, Inc., New York.

RANDOM HOUSE and colophon are registered trademarks of Random House, Inc.

Grateful acknowledgment is made to the following for permission
to reprint previously published material:
Alfred Publishing Co., Inc.: Excerpt from "Light One Candle"
by Peter Yarrow, copyright © 1982 by Silver Dawn Music. All rights reserved.
Reprinted by permission of Alfred Publishing Co., Inc.

www.randomhouse.com/kids

Educators and librarians, for a variety of teaching tools, visit us at
www.randomhouse.com/teachers

Library of Congress Cataloging-in-Publication Data
Bauer, A.C.E.
No castles here / A.C.E. Bauer. — 1st ed.
p. cm.
SUMMARY: Eleven-year-old Augie Boretski dreams of escaping his run-down
Camden, New Jersey, neighborhood, but things start to turn around with help from
a Big Brother, a music teacher, and a mysterious bookstore owner, so when his
school is in trouble, he pulls the community together to save it.
ISBN 978-0-375-83921-4 (trade) — ISBN 978-0-375-93921-1 (lib. bdg.)
[1. Determination (personality trait)—Fiction.   2. City and town life—New Jersey—
Camden—Fiction.   3. Books and reading—Fiction.   4. Choirs (Music)—Fiction.
5. Magic—Fiction.   6. Camden (N.J.)—Fiction.]   I. Title.
PZ7.B3257No   2007   [Fic]—dc22   2006023601

Printed in the United States of America   10 9 8 7 6 5 4 3 2 1

First Edition

To
Herbert, Gila, and Jon—
for everything

Contents

Crossing the River   1

Donkey Gold   6

Thief!   11

Donkey Skin   17

Walter Jones   21

"Perfessor"   27

The Ring   34

Caught   41

The Fairy Godmother Takes Charge   47

A Visit to the Park   49

"Rich Boy"   57

From Bad to Worse   66

To the Rescue   72

To Build a Wooden Box   78

Stomachaches and Other Truths   80

Cutting Losses   88

Auditions   92

Cornered   101

At Louisa's   105

When Fairies Fall in Love   113

The Junior Chorus   119

Thanksgiving   126

Trapped Inside   135

Louisette de Bourgaille   139

Troubles   145

Louisa's Box   152

Jesse   162

The Square   171

The Horse Farm   178

Marie-Louise de Bourgaille Nordritch   190

School's Closed   200

A Look Inside   210

Supplies and Labor   217

The Last of the Fairy Godmothers   228

Shedding the Donkey Skin   238

The Chorus Gets to Work   244

Sergio, Down   251

At the Board of Education   255

Not Taking "No" for an Answer   263

NO CASTLES
HERE

Crossing the River

AUGIE BORETSKI SNUCK OUT.

"Stay in," Mom had said before leaving for work. "I'll be home by six."

Stay in? On a super muggy, one-hundred-degree day in August? Their second-floor apartment had to be at least one hundred and twenty, even with the rickety fan going full blast.

The old lady downstairs stopped him as he opened the front door.

"Your mama, she worry."

Augie shrugged. What did Mrs. Lorentushki know, wearing her long-sleeved dress and flowery apron on a day like today?

1

"I'll be okay," he said before letting the screen door slam shut.

Besides, Mom didn't have to worry. He wasn't sticking around *this* neighborhood.

He counted the change in his bulging shorts pockets, checking one last time that he had enough to make it to Philly and back. He was getting out of here. Out of Camden. The armpit of the world, he thought, home to losers and drug dealers. Philadelphia sparkled across the Delaware River from the Camden waterfront. The buildings looked like castles, with spires and promise.

He walked the ten blocks to the Ferry Street station. At eleven in the morning, Augie didn't fear the gangs. He fed his coins to the ticket machine and boarded the train. He had escaped! Within minutes, he climbed out of the 13th Street station, ready to explore the big city without his mom there, fussing.

Walking down Locust Street, Augie passed one tall building after another, each looming above him like a fortress with its drawbridge up. Cars zoomed past, but except for one man in a business suit and one woman in a crisp dress, the sidewalks were empty. The buildings became shorter and turned to brick. Waves of heat rose from the concrete. Then he noticed the side streets.

Unlike the wide avenues he'd been crossing, these side streets were narrow, with small gardens, gnarled trees, and sometimes a barbecue grill. He turned into one full of shade. Shiny white teeth peeked out from a store window.

White teeth?

He stared at the display. The teeth belonged to a large toy donkey, with round eyes and a red-and-gold blanket on its back. The animal brayed at a doll dressed like a princess, who crouched to pick flowers. Curiosity pulled him into the shop.

After the door closed behind him with a tinkling of bells, Augie realized that he should have paid more attention to the books he had seen at the princess's feet. What was he going to do in a bookstore?

He spun around, lifted his arm to pull the door open, and paused. He felt his wet T-shirt unpeel from his back. His neck prickled as beads of sweat cooled in the air-conditioning. Nice. He could use a break from the sun. He let his arm drop and turned back around. What *was* he going to do in a bookstore?

He'd never been in a bookstore before. There were none in his Camden neighborhood. The closest shop was a bodega two blocks away that cashed checks and sold milk and bread. Aspirin and razor blades were kept behind bulletproof Plexiglas, along with cigarettes. Augie never hung around there—the owner rushed people in and out, saying, "This ain't no museum."

This bookstore was entirely different.

It had an unhurried quiet that Augie liked. The

quiet wasn't awful, like in the classroom when everyone prayed someone else was going to be called upon. There was no edge to this quiet. People moved about, minding their own business, at ease with each other.

"Thank you, Louisa," a customer said to a tall African American woman with her dark hair pulled into a knot. She smiled, and her gray eyes shifted for a second and focused on Augie.

Augie ducked into an aisle. He didn't want to be noticed. He had gone only a few paces when he saw a deep chair with enormous cushions in faded black leather. On its seat lay a dark green book with gold letters etched into the cover. He lifted the book, sank into the chair, and pushed his glasses back up his nose. *Aaah . . .* He looked up. On the wall next to him hung a yellowed picture of a dignified African American gentleman in a three-piece suit with a straw hat and a cane. He sat under a tree next to a stately white woman in a long, pale lace dress, her hair piled up high with a tiny hat perched forward on top of her head. They stared at him, as if amused by his presence.

"What are you looking at?" Augie asked them.

The shopkeeper seemed to answer him: "I have several volumes covering mollusks over here."

She was leading a customer in Augie's direction. He opened the book he still held, as if he were interested. Maybe she wouldn't notice him with his nose buried in a book.

Augie didn't like to read. He read whatever he was told to read at school—most of the time. At home, he watched the few TV channels they could catch, or sang along with music on the radio. They didn't own any real books—none that he remembered.

But something odd happened when he cracked open that green spine. The very first page had a picture of the braying donkey from the store window, but this time it held its tail high. It pooped golden coins into a silver bowl held by a king in crimson robes. The princess was nowhere to be seen.

Awesome!

He turned the page. The first letter of the first word was an elaborate *L* with green vines all around it and a donkey head peeking out from behind it. The words were crisp black on a creamy white. He touched them with the tips of his fingers. It made no sense. They almost felt alive.

Augie was eleven and a half. This was his time for adventure. He hadn't figured it would begin in a bookstore.

He started reading.

DONKEY GOLD

LONG AGO AND FAR AWAY, a great and powerful king owned a donkey that he treasured beyond all other possessions. Instead of manure, the donkey produced gold, and so the kingdom was always wealthy. One day the king's wife died, and he was left with a young daughter, Annette. The king had loved his queen dearly and was grieved by her loss. He could not bear to see anything that reminded him of her, especially not their beautiful young princess. So Annette was sent off to the far recesses of the castle, to be cared for by her fairy godmother, who had instructions never to allow the girl within eyesight of the king.

The king grieved for fifteen years while his counselors fretted.

"You need a male heir," they told him, "and a queen to produce one."

The king finally relented. He agreed to remarry.

"But on one condition," he said. "My new bride must be as beautiful and as intelligent as my dear departed wife."

The court searched far and wide, but for naught. The king dismissed one eligible woman after another as not being beautiful or intelligent enough.

One spring morning, the king decided to take a walk in his gardens. This futile search for a wife was tiresome. Why couldn't his court understand that he didn't want to remarry? Then, as he fretted, he caught sight of the most beautiful maiden he had ever seen. She was cutting flowers and laying them in a basket while humming to herself. Her motions were as fluid as a mountain stream, her face fresher than a rose, and her voice more melodious than a nightingale's. The king was thunderstruck. His empty heart filled with desire. This was the maid he wanted to marry! The king ran to the gardener.

"Tell me," he commanded, "who is the fair lady picking flowers in my gardens?"

"Your daughter, Your Majesty," the gardener answered. "Princess Annette."

In the fifteen years of mourning, the king had not laid eyes upon his daughter. He had not seen the child grow into a woman. Her sudden appearance overwhelmed him, and all his sense flew away. He ordered that they should be married the very next day.

The court was appalled. A father marry his own child? This could not be done. But no one was able to dissuade the king.

"I am your ruler!" the king roared. "You must do as I command!"

Annette was repelled by the notion. She pleaded with her father to change his mind. But he was steadfast. In her despair she ran to her fairy godmother, Louisa, for advice.

Louisa was both ancient and wise. She had loved and cared for the king's wife while she was alive, and had devoted herself completely to Annette after the queen's death. Although Louisa wielded magic, she knew that only the king could change his own heart.

"The shock of seeing you has sent him reeling," she told Annette. "In time, he shall see the nature of his folly. We must find a way to delay."

At Louisa's urging, the princess requested an audience with the king.

"I shall marry," the princess said, "but I require a trousseau."

The king was surprised. He was giving her away to himself. She did not need to bring dresses and linens to a new home. But he was smitten by his child and so he nodded in agreement.

"In my trousseau I would like a gown that rivals the summer sky in splendor."

"Anything you desire!" he said.

Using his magic donkey's gold, he hired the greatest spinners, the craftiest weavers, and the most careful tailors to make a gown that should rival the summer sky in splendor.

After six months of continuous work, the craftspeople had harnessed silver and sapphires, lapis and pearls, satins and silks. They wove the petals of violets, captured the reflection of a quiet pool, and created a gown of sweet sky blue, with a hint of a summer breeze that rippled across the fabric and disappeared. When Annette donned her dress, she glowed like the sky!

"It is perfect, my daughter. Now we shall marry," the king said.

"My trousseau is incomplete, my dear father," Annette replied. "I have a gown for the day, but none for the night."

The king fumed. But he had promised her anything she desired. And so he called back the weary craftspeople and ordered a gown for his daughter that should rival the night sky.

Another six months passed. This time they collected the silk of spiderwebs and the evening dew from the grass. They spun ebony with ivory, and onyx with diamonds, wove the finest white lace with perfect moonstones, and created a gown of deep black that twinkled with stars and shone like the full moon. When Annette wore the gown, all of the king's court gasped at this vision of the night sky.

A year had passed, yet the king's ardor had only increased. He pressed for a wedding day. Annette persevered.

"My father, you have done as I have asked. But a bride requires a wedding dress. It needs to shine, my father, more brilliantly than the sun itself!"

The king shook his head but relented.

"Very well, you shall have this dress. But do you promise me that it shall be the last one that you ask for?"

When Annette agreed, the king called his craftspeople and ordered a new gown, one more brilliant than the sun itself.

The spinners and weavers and tailors were exhausted. But the king had commanded, so they set to work for another six months. This time they collected the yellow firelight from beeswax candles and honey fresh from the comb. They spun gold and topaz, fire opal and gypsum, saffron and turmeric, and the shimmer from ripe wheatfields. And when they were near collapse, they presented their creation to the princess. The dress was beyond compare. When Annette entered the king's court, all had to shade their eyes from the brilliance of her gown. Warmth radiated with her every movement. Her father exulted.

"The wedding shall be tomorrow," he announced.

Annette was at a loss. The plan had failed. What should she do? She ran to find her fairy godmother.

Thief!

A HUGE ORANGE CAT leaped on the arm of Augie's chair, jolting Augie out of his reading. Cats always spooked him: they snuck around and stared at him as if they planned on attacking him when he wasn't paying attention.

"Down, boy," he whispered.

The cat ignored him and washed itself. Augie wasn't taking any chances. He climbed out of the chair sideways, slowly, so that the beast wouldn't jump on him. Then Augie left in a hurry.

He had run two blocks before he realized he was still clutching the green book. He stopped dead in his tracks, unsure of what to do next.

He felt torn. He hadn't paid for it. If there was one lesson Mom had drilled into him since he was old enough to remember, it was to never, ever steal. He'd turn around, he told himself. Go back to the store and return the book. But he hadn't finished the story!

He shook his head. Since when did he read fairy tales? Nothing in those stories resembled his life, not even remotely. His mom was a waitress at the Pear Hill Diner, not some queen. They lived in a yellow two-story row house in Camden, New Jersey, no castle, that was for sure. And as much as he'd like it, no gold-pooping donkey hung around their neighborhood.

Yet this story wrapped itself around him, sank into his chest, filled his brain. He wanted to know more. It reminded him of the feeling he always got when he listened to a song with a great tune, one that kept repeating itself in his head. He had to learn the verses, all of them, from beginning to end, before he could let the song go. He needed to finish this story.

Augie looked down at the dark green volume, a bit wilted now in his sweaty palms. A police car passed him.

The lady at the store must have figured him for a thief! He ducked into the nearest subway station to catch the train across the Delaware. He didn't want trouble.

He felt anxious the entire ride home. Did the

wrinkled Asian lady with the big mesh bag know he held stolen goods? What about the teenage couple in the corner who wore enough gold between them to light up a room?

Augie smiled. Is that what the princess's sun dress looked like?

He glanced down at the book he hugged to his chest and loosened his grip. The cover decompressed and the pages expanded, as if they were taking a breath.

Augie sighed. Why didn't teachers ever give him anything like this to read at school?

School sucked. Augie never did well, and his teachers ignored him. He wasn't smart, he wasn't stupid, and he wasn't a troublemaker. But the real problem, Augie had to admit, was Dwaine.

Dwaine Malloy had moved to Camden when Augie was seven. As the only two white kids in their grade, they had been placed in the same class ever since—as if they had anything in common.

Augie was short and skinny, with brown eyes hidden behind thick glasses. He spent most of his time trying to be invisible. He had managed to make one friend, Tyler Brown, a kid with a lazy eye but with a smile that filled a room. They kept to themselves, mostly.

Dwaine was three times as wide as Augie and at least a head taller. He had beady blue eyes and wiry orange hair that stood straight out. He used his fearsome

looks to his advantage: he didn't try to fit in, or hide—
he was the class bully. Augie was his favorite target.
Augie had lost track of how often Dwaine had punched
him in the arm as they passed each other in the hallway.
He mashed gum in Augie's hair, tripped him at every
opportunity, and gave him wedgies "just for practice."
And if Augie didn't hand over something he wanted,
right away, he walloped him good.

Tyler did try to stick up for Augie. And sometimes, Dwaine backed off. But the Brown family moved
away. Without Tyler there, no one wanted to side with
Augie.

Augie had avoided Dwaine all summer. But school
started in a few days, and Augie knew his misery was
about to begin once again.

What if Dwaine caught him with a book? Of fairy
tales, no less?

Augie ran the ten long blocks from the train stop
to his house. Now that his pockets were no longer
weighed down by coins for the train fare, he let loose.
With a solid grip on the book, he raced past the boarded-
up shopping center and crossed over an alley filled with
garbage, avoiding the drug dealers' park altogether. He
was breathing hard when he slipped the key into the
front door of their row house.

"You were away a long time," Mrs. Lorentushki said.

She had opened her apartment door as soon as he

stepped into the hallway. Augie wiped the sweat off his forehead.

"Mom won't be home till six," he mumbled.

The old lady tsk-tsked but gave Augie an apple.

"Growing boys need vitamins," she said.

Augie nodded a thanks and sprinted up the stairs. He could feel her eyeing the book. It became heavier somehow. Even within the safety of their apartment, away from prying eyes, the book weighed on him. He placed it on their Formica table.

What was Augie going to do now? He absentmindedly turned on the radio that sat on the counter and began humming along with the tune. He needed to think, but his rumbling stomach distracted him. He smelled something delicious wafting up from the old lady's kitchen. Man, was he hungry—too hungry to concentrate! He reached for the apple next to the book, picked both up, and sank into the old recliner.

He'd hide the book. There must be somewhere in the apartment Mom wouldn't look. Nestled in his lap, the green volume seemed precious. The pages had flared open a bit. Augie opened the cover to the picture at the front.

It had changed! Now a woman wore a donkey pelt over her shoulders, the donkey's head had become her cap, and she fed slop to filthy pigs. How could this be? He flipped the pages back and forth. Had he imagined the first picture? Or did he remember wrong? No. He knew what he had seen. The king with the silver bowl and gold-pooping donkey were gone. They had been replaced—how, he did not know.

He stared at the woman and pigs a second longer, then flipped the pages forward. Maybe the book would explain it to him.

DONKEY SKIN

When Princess Annette found her fairy godmother, she wept. Their plan had failed. The king had summoned the entire court to prepare for tomorrow's wedding.

"All is not lost," her godmother reassured her.

She whispered into Annette's ear. The princess shuddered but returned to the bustling throne room.

"Annette," the king said, "a bride should rest before the wedding. Why are you here?"

"My trousseau is complete," Annette replied, "and I thank you for your generosity. But still, I would like a wedding present from the groom."

"Anything," the king replied, "so long as it can be acquired today."

"It can," Annette said, her head bowed.

"Speak," the king demanded.

"I desire the skin from your magic donkey."

Silence descended upon the court. Everyone knew how much the king loved the donkey. Only his most trusted servants were allowed near it. It lived in the grandest quarters in the castle and ate the best foods. The king trembled with horror. He pleaded in vain. The princess knew that this request was the only way to stop him. She was sure he would refuse.

But Annette had not fathomed the depth of his folly. That evening, there was a knock at her bedchamber door. When her fairy godmother, Louisa, opened it, the king entered with the skin of his beloved donkey.

"It is done," he said before leaving.

What had Annette accomplished? The poor beast, who had only served his master faithfully, was now dead because of her. And her father still persisted in his insane desire. She despaired. Her fairy godmother shook her head in dismay.

"He is truly mad. You must run, disguised as the lowest of the low."

She cast a spell. The reeking donkey's skin lifted itself up and wrapped itself around the princess. The fairy waved her wand once more, and grime covered the princess's face, while dirty clogs replaced the dainty slippers on her feet.

"Follow my wand," Louisa instructed, "and you will reach a farm. There you will be employed as a keeper of pigs."

The princess cried at this, but the fairy was firm.

"You cannot marry your father. After you flee, he will search for you everywhere, but he will not look among the swineherds."

The fairy loved her goddaughter, so she cast another spell. The contents of the princess's bedroom folded into a small wooden box.

"In the forest, near the farm, you will find an empty cottage. After you have bolted the door and shuttered the windows, open this box that I am lending you, and the contents of your room shall fill the cottage. You will also be able to summon any other object you may need from the box. But go, now, before it dawns on the king that you might leave."

Wearing the foul donkey skin, Princess Annette fled the palace under the cover of night, her godmother's magic wand lighting her path. After a long night and several more days and nights of travel, the wand vanished. The princess had reached a hardscrabble farm run by an old woman, neither friendly nor cruel, who nodded to the heartbroken princess.

"Return at daybreak," the woman said. "The pigs will want to be fed."

In the days and weeks that followed, the old woman asked Donkey Skin, as the princess was now called, to do the hardest work, the dirtiest jobs. The donkey's pelt became dirtier and dirtier, and Donkey Skin no longer needed the fairy's magic to appear slovenly. Farmworkers and townsfolk avoided her wherever she went—she was ugly, and she stank.

But when her day's chores were complete, Donkey Skin returned to her cottage, locked the door, shuttered the windows, and opened the magic box. The donkey's pelt fell away, and Annette became clean once again. She donned one of her dresses and for a little while felt like the princess that she was. Sometimes, when her day had been particularly hard, she propped a hand mirror against a kettle hanging low in her fireplace. Then she could see all of herself—if she stood across the room. She pretended that she was back in the castle gardens tending the flowers.

Walter Jones

AUGIE DIDN'T HEAR THE downstairs door open. From halfway up the stairs, his mom yelled, "I'm home!" Augie realized he had better hide the book, fast, or he'd have some tough explaining to do.

He reached behind the couch that doubled as his bed and pulled out a large shoe box. It contained about a dozen comic books that he had collected over the years along with four pennies, all the money he had left after his trip to Philly. His mom never looked there. He wedged the dark green book between Batman and Spider-Man, shoved the box behind the couch, and switched on the TV.

When his mom walked into the apartment, Augie pretended to watch the news.

"I brought some fruit salad," she said.

Augie took a breath and smiled. The syrupy fruit salad Mom got from the diner was his favorite dessert. It tasted like liquid candy. He almost felt like he didn't deserve the treat.

He watched her remove a couple of day-old bagels and some bologna wrapped in plastic from her bag. These were also from the diner—their supper. She was like the princess—special within, but working a hard, thankless job without. He wondered whether she'd be more like a princess if she wore less of that makeup she used to cover her face. She was pretty, he thought, with her large brown eyes and light brown hair, even when her hair was pulled back into her waitress ponytail. When he was smaller, he would catch her in the morning, before she "put her face on," as she said, and snuggle next to her in her bed.

"You're a prince," she always said.

Didn't that make her royalty, too?

Royal or not, Mom didn't seem hungry tonight. Augie had almost finished his meal before she nibbled even a bit.

"The Big Brother program called," she said. "They've found a match."

The bottom fell out of Augie's stomach.

"I've told you," Augie said. "I'm too old for a Big Brother."

"My job keeps me busy," Mom replied. "This'll be someone who can take you places."

"I don't need some grown-up dragging me around. And I don't want anyone nosing into my business."

Mom persisted. "It'll be nice to have someone else in your life."

That was, of course, what this argument was all about. Mom always wanted to get him involved with other people, especially since Tyler moved away.

When Augie was nine, she signed him up with a Cub Scout pack all the way over in Pear Hill. One of the pack mothers worked with Mom and had talked her into it. She even agreed to pick him up for the meetings. Augie attended until the father-and-son campout. Everyone was excited. The pack leader had borrowed sleeping bags for all the boys, and they were to spend a night at some park near the Pine Barrens. But Augie didn't have anyone to take him: he had no father, or uncle, or grandpa to go with. He never signed up—didn't even show the papers to Mom. What was the point? He stopped going to Cub Scouts after that. Mom was disappointed, but Augie had never liked it. He stuck out: the other boys had known each other since kindergarten, while he was the uncoordinated, skinny kid from the mean city. He was picked last for every activity, or ended up being the odd kid without a partner—the one the pack leader had to keep company. Augie had tensed up before each meeting. Not going was an enormous relief.

But this Big Brother business seemed to mean so much to Mom that Augie relented.

"I'll only do it once," he said. "No promises."

Mom agreed.

The next day Mom took him to the Big Brother office downtown. She had made him change into a shirt with buttons and comb his stringy brown hair. Great. He looked like a geek.

The social worker was waiting for them in her office. Augie wondered where she had gotten all those books and papers that seemed to fill every corner of the tiny room.

"Walter Jones is eager to meet you," she told Augie.

"Augie's eager, too," Mom said.

Hadn't Mom always told him not to lie? Augie slid low in his chair. He wished he could just disappear.

The social worker looked down at some papers on her desk. "Walter owns a greenhouse in Pear Hill. He grows organic vegetables." She looked up again and gave a thousand-watt smile. "I bet he'll be interesting to talk to."

Augie slid lower. Mom and the social worker exchanged glances.

"I'm sure they'll get along," Mom said.

The social worker's smile stayed painted on. "He's in the back office. Why don't I bring him over?" She rose and headed down the hall.

"Come on," Mom whispered. "You said you'd behave."

Augie frowned but sat up straighter.

An organic farmer, Augie thought. He was hooked up with a stupid organic farmer! Some do-gooder who'd try to convince Augie that the world should be kept green. What did this guy know about living in a city like Camden?

"Glad to meet you, Augie," a deep voice said.

Augie looked up at a tall, powerful, blond-haired man who extended a huge hand toward him. Augie hesitated before sticking out his arm. The man's hand swallowed his as they shook and said hello.

"Want to come see my truck?" Walter Jones asked.

Augie glanced at Mom and the social worker, who were nodding. He shrugged.

"Okay."

As Augie followed Walter outside, he felt even smaller and goofier than usual. People always mistook him for someone younger than he was, and standing next to Walter Jones wasn't going to help.

At least the pickup was cool. Big, shiny, and silver, it felt solid. It didn't look slick, like the kind office workers from the suburbs drove, with bulging fenders Augie figured came from slipping steroids into the fuel. It didn't look like the kind city workers drove, either: worn out, beaten up, and dirty. Walter's was a truck without fluff. It looked like it hauled heavy stuff daily, while being well maintained. Someone respected this machine.

Augie couldn't help himself. "Nice wheels!"

The tall man smiled. "She gets me where I need to go."

Augie circled the pickup, taking note of the large-tread tires, the slightly scuffed running board, the bumpers that gleamed. Sandwiched between a small blue Ford and a rusty Toyota, it stood out. If the kids in the neighborhood saw him in this, maybe he'd get some respect!

"Could I ride in it sometime?" Augie asked.

"Sure thing. How about I pick you up Sunday?"

Augie nodded.

But as soon as they walked back into the social worker's office, he regretted his decision. What would people say when a Big Brother showed up at his house, as if he were some little kid?

"Perfessor"

ON HIS FIRST DAY of sixth grade, Augie discovered that not only had Dwaine been assigned to his class, but so had Sergio Barnaby and Fox Tooth Green. Someone must have fallen asleep in the administration office to have placed the three biggest troublemakers at Willard Elementary into one classroom.

Sergio's good-looking presence scared Augie worse than Dwaine's ugly one. Sergio was smart and mean and didn't go anywhere without Fox Tooth, his dark, oily flunky. Fox Tooth's real name was Thomas, but because of his pointy teeth, someone had given him the nickname in kindergarten, and now no one but teachers called him anything else. The rumor was that Sergio and Fox Tooth had collected more lunch money from kids in one month last year than anyone else in the entire history of Willard Elementary School.

To make matters worse, Mr. Franklin and Ms. Lewis were Augie's teachers. Ms. Lewis, who taught language arts and science, was okay, but Mr. Franklin was the meanest, toughest teacher in school. He had been the school's music instructor, but a few years ago the school ran out of money, so they cut all the art and music programs. When one of the sixth-grade teachers retired, they asked Mr. Franklin to take over. He had been teaching sixth-grade math and social studies ever since.

Most kids were afraid of him. He was an imposing figure, over six feet tall, built like a linebacker, with closely cropped black hair. Everyone had heard the story of how Mr. Franklin had once thrown a kid out of a window when the boy didn't show up properly dressed for a chorus recital. No one messed with Mr. Franklin.

Augie knew he was in deep trouble. This was confirmed at lunchtime. Sergio and Fox Tooth cornered him in the hallway.

"If it ain't Augustus," Sergio said.

Fox Tooth grinned, showing off a double set of very pointy teeth.

"Your glasses are slidin' down your nose. Want me to push 'em up?"

Augie started to back away, but Dwaine came up from behind.

"Don't want to lose them, do you?" he said. "Need 'em to read your special book."

"Augustus got a book?" Sergio said.

"Held it close," Dwaine mock-whispered, "like it was precious."

Dwaine had seen him when he had run home. Damn!

"It's just a book," Augie said.

"No need to be snooty 'bout it, Perfessor," Sergio said.

"Maybe we take him down a notch," Dwaine said.

Sergio and Fox Tooth exchanged glances. At that moment the tall, dark brown figure of Mr. Franklin came upon them.

"Mr. Malloy, may I have a word?"

Augie escaped, but he saw the glares the boys sent his way. They planned to get even. That afternoon he ran home faster than ever. He feared every dark alley, every corner.

The next day, Mr. Franklin announced that he had created a seating chart.

"I like to know where everyone will be."

He placed Dwaine, Fox Tooth, and Sergio in three of the corners. Augie lucked out. He was only a desk away from the door.

"When I assign homework," Mr. Franklin continued, "I expect it to be turned in. If you don't, I'll assume it's because you have no time to complete it at home." His eyes narrowed. "That being the case, I'll make time for you."

On Thursday, everyone found out what that meant. Sergio and Fox Tooth were kept after the last bell.

"Until you finish today's assignments," Mr. Franklin told them.

Augie saw Dwaine hanging around the schoolyard, waiting for them. They had, to his dismay, become a threesome. But for the first time all week, Augie wasn't out of breath when he crossed his threshold.

Mrs. Lorentushki stood at her door.

"Growing boys need vitamins," she said, handing Augie a banana.

"Thanks," Augie said.

He enjoyed his bit of peace that afternoon. He sang, better than any tune on the radio, while he did his schoolwork at the kitchen table. But he knew his luck wouldn't last forever. Even bullies could figure out how to do a half-assed job on assignments so that they wouldn't be held after school. He had to come up with some better way to avoid them or he'd be sprinting home every single day of the year.

Friday after lunch, Sergio started a game of "Tag the Perfessor," the goal being to knock Augie's glasses off. Augie had been run ragged around the playground, and they were closing in. Augie decided to break school rules and hide inside. He ran downstairs, at least twenty feet ahead of Dwaine, zoomed past the lockers, and saw a door at the end of the hall opened a crack. He ducked in and shut the door.

He had found the old music room. They stored chairs and desks in it now, but by the look of it, someone still used it. The teacher's desk was clear of dust and had a lit lamp on it. Augie expected someone to turn up at any moment, but the bell rang, and he made it back to class unharmed.

Dwaine sent him evil stares from across the room all afternoon. Augie buried his nose in his notebook. They were going to massacre him at the end of the day! A minute before the bell, he stuffed all his books into his bag. Before the ring faded, he sprinted out and ran downstairs. He hid again in the music room.

He spent an anxious fifteen minutes listening to kids down the hall slam their lockers. The bustle died down, and soon there was nothing but silence. Augie waited another fifteen minutes. They might be out front. Another fifteen minutes. They might be waiting at the park.

He watched the big round clock on the wall tick away. He was certain that Dwaine, Sergio, and Fox Tooth were lying in ambush at his house. But he was getting hungry, holed up in there, and he longed for one of those pieces of fruit Mrs. Lorentushki always gave him. Outside was quiet. Maybe they had given up. But what if they hadn't? Another fifteen minutes, he decided. Two minutes later, someone pushed open the door to the music room.

Mr. Franklin!

"Augustus! What are you doing here?"

Augie felt himself redden. "It's a quiet place for homework."

Mr. Franklin must have known this was a lie. Augie's bag lay unopened at his feet. But if Mr. Franklin knew, he chose to ignore it.

"I was locking up," he said. "You'd better head home now."

Augie nodded and reached for his bag.

"You can come in here to work anytime," Mr. Franklin added. "I've kept the keys."

Augie said "thanks" without looking at Mr. Franklin's face and left. Not a soul was around.

"Late today," Mrs. Lorentushki said. Worry had crept into her voice.

"Special assignment from my teacher," Augie told her.

The explanation seemed to suffice. She smiled and offered a plum.

"You're the best," Augie said, climbing the stairs to his apartment.

Maybe he hadn't lied to Mrs. Lorentushki, he thought. The music room was a great place to hide. And Mr. Franklin had told him he could use it. Once word got around that it was Mr. Franklin's office, no one was going to mess with the space. Augie'd be safer there than in the principal's office.

Mom was working the late shift today. "More tips," she had told him. He bit into the plum. She had left him a sandwich and carrot sticks in the fridge for dinner, but they didn't tempt him.

Augie sighed. The apartment felt emptier than usual.

The radio seemed to make the emptiness worse. The DJ was a stranger in Philadelphia and sounded as lonely as Augie felt. Augie switched him off and turned on the TV. He had the choice between several versions of the news, a rerun he had seen too often, and a cooking show. He switched that off, too. That's when he remembered the book.

He pulled the sofa out a bit, just enough to reach behind it, rummaged in the box, and took the book out. It felt heavier, somehow, and maybe thicker. He shook his head. He opened to the front page—the picture was different, once again! A prince sat in an ornate bed, his shirt loose, his hair rumpled around his thin crown. He stared intently at a ring with a large, smooth white stone in it. The stone almost twinkled on the page. Augie touched it, and it felt cold, as if it were real. A shiver tingled down his spine. He turned the page, and the book opened to the exact spot where he had left off.

Augie grinned.

THE RING

ONTHS PASSED FOR DONKEY SKIN. And a year. Life took on a routine, morning till dusk. Donkey Skin was a swineherd. No more. No less. Then one day, a party of hunters rode into the hardscrabble farm. These were noble young men who had become lost in the forest mist. They were hungry and tired, and they asked for shelter.

The old woman who ran the farm was gracious, in her way. She found the best of everything she had, and she fed them well with fresh foods and hearty wine. She laid out some cots and offered her feather bed to the finest young man of them all, Prince François from the neighboring kingdom.

Donkey Skin watched the hunters that evening, from a distance. She was not allowed to approach so fine a party, but she noticed the prince's demeanor. He treated all of his attendants as equals and gave each an opportunity to shine. He was kind to the gruff old woman and thoughtful of the tired page who tended his horse. When Donkey Skin departed for her cottage, she wished she could meet this young gentleman.

Unaware of either Donkey Skin's presence or her departure, the young noblemen reveled until late that evening. When they finally went to bed, the prince could not fall asleep. He tossed and turned and eventually decided to go for a walk. He had not gone far when he found Donkey Skin's cottage. The door was shut and the windows were shuttered, but light shone from the chimney. He was intrigued. He put his ear to the door, and he heard a plaintive song. The voice was melodious and seemed to shoot right through his heart. Who sang such a beautiful and sad melody?

The prince tried to look through the shutters, but they were too tight. There were no cracks in the door. He looked up. The chimney, after all, had brought him to this place. So he climbed the thatch roof and reached the chimney pot. When the prince looked down, he saw, reflected in a mirror, a princess in a dress bluer and brighter than the summer sky. It radiated warm light. The vision overwhelmed him.

He did not sleep that night. He stayed upon the roof, hoping to catch another glimpse of the princess, until all went dark and he realized that the lovely maid must have gone to bed. He roamed around the cottage, trying to find hints about who lived there.

What the prince did not know was that Donkey Skin had heard him on the roof. After she turned out the light, she cracked open her shutters. By the light of the full moon, she watched him pace around the cottage. What a fine figure! What a fine face!

But she could not step out of the cottage to meet him—not as a princess. Only as Donkey Skin.

The prince returned to the farm at daybreak, faint from fatigue. His courtiers were beside themselves with worry. They were convinced the woods harbored some evil that must have swallowed him at night. When he reappeared, they were so happy to see him that they almost carried him away, then and there, back to the safety of their realm.

"Wait," ordered the prince. "I must speak with the woman who runs the farm." The old woman came forward. "Tell me, grandmother, who is the maiden who lives in the cottage up beyond the path?"

The old woman almost doubled over with laughter.

"Maiden?" she said. "I have heard Donkey Skin called many names, but *maiden* isn't one of them."

Before anything more could be said, the noblemen whisked their prince back through the forest, to the palace.

When Prince François arrived home, he was sick with longing for Donkey Skin. His courtiers, who had caught glimpses of Donkey Skin at the farm, could not believe their fine prince had fallen in love with such an ugly and foul-smelling person. The king and queen were worried: the prince ate less and less, and nothing tempted his appetite. He took to his bed. Doctors and wise folk were called, but none could cure him.

"What shall we do, my son?" the queen asked. "You must eat."

"I will eat," said the prince. "But only a cake made by Donkey Skin."

The king and queen immediately gave the order, and a page was sent back to the hardscrabble farm. There he found Donkey Skin.

"I have been instructed to ask you to bake a cake for His Royal Highness, Prince François, and I am not to leave until you have given it to me."

The old woman who ran the farm shook her head in wonder.

"You heard him," she said to Donkey Skin. "Get to work."

Donkey Skin was overjoyed. This was her chance to send a message to the prince. But how, she wondered. A finely written letter given to the page would raise eyebrows: no swineherd knew how to write. She had to send her message through the cake.

She ran to her cottage, bolted the door, shuttered the windows, and shed the horrid donkey's skin. She opened the magic box and dressed in her gown of the night.

"A recipe," she whispered, "a recipe for a lover's cake!"

Lo and behold, a bowl, a spoon, butter, milk, flour, and everything else she needed floated from the box, and quickly the batter took shape. From her right hand she removed a perfect moonstone ring, washed it tenderly, and dropped it into the ready pans. In an hour the cake was baked. She iced it carefully in yellow and white, then placed it on a crystal platter with a crystal cover on top.

The princess put on the donkey skin. The crystal turned to wood, and not a trace of Donkey Skin's regal appearance remained. The page could not believe that the prince wanted a cake made by such a disgusting creature. But he did as he had been instructed. With great care, he brought the cake back to the prince.

The king and queen were appalled by the grimy wooden receptacle the page carried. The prince, however, was enthralled.

"Bring it to my chambers," he ordered.

The cake was set on a table, and the prince dismissed everyone from his room. As soon as he touched the wooden cover, it turned back into crystal. He lifted it and admired the beautiful cake. He cut himself a slice. As he bit into it, he almost broke a tooth: he had discovered the ring!

For hours, Prince François admired the ring. He kissed its perfect moonstone. It was a message, he knew. He summoned the king and queen.

"I have been heartsick," he told them. "The cure will be my wedding."

The king and queen were overjoyed. Long had they desired grandchildren to carry on their lineage. The prince pulled out the ring.

"Whoever's finger fits this ring shall be my bride."

A proclamation was sent, far and wide: Prince François was to marry the maiden, any maiden, who could wear the moonstone ring. Princesses, noblewomen, and peasants' daughters queued up on the assigned morning. By order of the king and queen, they were lined up by rank. Surely, someone of nobility, they thought, would fit the ring first.

But of course this was not so. On some, the ring was too big. On others, it was too small. It fit no one. As the maids wound their way down the long line, the prince patiently tried to place the ring on each outstretched hand. Though a great many of the women had beauty and grace, none matched the vision the prince had seen through the chimney.

Evening fell. Lamps were lit. Still the prince kept trying to fit the ring. All of the women of noble birth had failed. So had the common women. The last maid had just been dismissed when a commotion came from the palace entrance.

"You may not enter," a guard cried.

"But all maidens may appear," a voice replied.

The prince stood. He recognized the voice as the one he had heard sing through the cottage door.

"Let her in," he commanded.

A guard came in with Donkey Skin at arm's length. The assembly gasped. She was so filthy, so smelly, so ugly, so altogether revolting, no one wanted to be near her.

"You are Donkey Skin?" the prince inquired.

Donkey Skin curtsied deep and reverentially.

"Come," he said.

The courtiers did not believe their eyes, nor their ears. How could their beloved prince even tolerate Donkey Skin being in the same room as himself? Donkey Skin approached the throne. The king and queen averted their eyes and held their noses. But the prince walked down to meet her. He smiled into her eyes, and she smiled back. He lifted her tarred and oily hand and took the ring from his pocket. It slipped easily, perfectly, completely onto her ring finger. His smile grew.

"No!" gasped the queen.

To everyone's horror, the prince bowed down and kissed the hand of the beast.

Time held its breath. The donkey skin fell to the floor. Princess Annette stood before the court, shining more brilliantly than the sun itself. The royal pair were married that very night.

Caught

AUGIE LIFTED HIS HEAD for a moment, trying to imagine this royal wedding, when he heard the downstairs door slam shut.

Those were Mom's footsteps. She was at least two hours early.

Augie scrambled to hide the book, but the stupid thing had become a lead weight, getting heavier and heavier in his lap. He used every ounce of effort he had to close it. When he tried to lift it, it slipped and landed on the floor with a crash. Mom walked in just at that moment.

"What was that?" she asked.

Augie didn't answer. He stared down at the floor.

In two steps, she was over to the couch. She swooped the book up in one motion. Why didn't *she* have any trouble lifting it?

"*Donkey Skin and Other Tales,*" she read. "Retold and Expanded by Louisa Nordritch."

She arched her eyebrows.

"Schoolbook?"

Augie had just been handed a perfect out. Yet as much as he wanted to, and he wanted to very much, he was unable to lie to his mother. He hadn't had trouble lying to her before. What was the matter with him? He struggled to answer her, but nothing came out. Mom started to look worried.

"Why don't you tell me how you got this," she said.

Augie decided to concoct a story, any story. But, for no reason he could explain, he told her the truth instead. It just poured out. As he described his trip to the city, his venture into the bookstore, and the cat that had spooked him, he felt a knot that had been worrying him at the pit of his stomach begin to untie. Unfortunately, by the time he finished, Mom was furious.

"Not only did you sneak out when I told you to stay in, but you went all the way to Philadelphia, and"—she waved the green volume—"you became a juvenile delinquent."

"It's a *book,* Mom," Augie protested.

"You stole it!"

"It was an accident."

Mom's eyebrows shot up even higher. She pronounced each syllable as if it were its own word. "Stealing is not an ac-ci-dent."

Augie wished he could shrink away. His mom looked so utterly disappointed.

"Tomorrow morning," she said, "we drive to your bookstore, and you are going to explain everything to the owner."

Augie quailed. But Mom wasn't finished.

"I'll lend you the money to pay for the book, but you're going to have to pay me back. And if the owner decides to prosecute, you take your lumps."

Augie felt miserable. He'd have been happy to go to jail at that very moment. Instead he had to spend the evening with Mom, who looked like she was going to either explode or cry. They both went to bed early.

The ride over the Ben Franklin Bridge the next morning in Mom's old Buick was very quiet. Augie noticed that Mom's eyes were red, even under the blue eye shadow she wore. Why did she have to wear so much? He spent his time staring out the window wishing that they'd never arrive. But they did. Mom found a parking space right away.

The street didn't seem anywhere near as enchanting as the first time Augie had seen it. To Augie's ears, the string of bells tinkled mournfully when they walked in.

"May we please speak to the owner?" Mom asked the African American woman at the cash register.

Augie recognized her from the first time he had been there.

"I am Louisa, the owner," the woman said.

Mom squeezed Augie's shoulder. "This young man has something to tell you."

Augie looked across the counter. The woman was tall and slim, with rich, amber-brown skin and black hair tied back in a knot. Her sharp nose and high forehead reminded him of an eagle. But her eyes were a liquid gray that seemed to go on forever.

He couldn't speak. She had recognized him, too, Augie could tell. Yet she smiled.

"It's about the book, isn't it?" she said.

Augie nodded. Mom took it out of her handbag and handed it to Augie, who slid it across the counter.

"I took it," he squeaked, "without paying for it."

Louisa's smile did not waver. If anything, it seemed friendlier. It gave Augie courage.

"I'd like to pay for it now."

"It's not for sale," she said.

There was a moment of silence while her words sank in. Mom stepped forward.

"Then we should reimburse you for the damage."

The book certainly didn't look new anymore. The cover wasn't smooth or flat, and the dark engraved vines along the borders seemed grubbier, somehow. The corners no longer had the crisp edge of a new book.

Louisa shook her head. Her eyes were sincere.

"It isn't damaged."

She opened it and gently flipped a few pages.

"The binding has not been harmed at all, and the pages are equally intact. The ripples on the cover have been there for ages."

Augie felt that this was too easy. After all, he had walked away with something that wasn't his.

"I'm sorry I took it," he said. "I shouldn't have."

The woman nodded.

"I'd like to make it up to you," Augie heard himself say. Why did he say that?

The woman now smiled like an old friend, pleased by a good piece of news.

"Finish the book," she said.

Augie couldn't believe what he had just heard. Apparently neither did Mom.

"You mean he should read it?"

The woman nodded. "Why don't you have a cup of coffee with me?" she said to Mom. "The young man can begin working on his reading in the meantime."

She pushed the book back in Augie's direction. Dazed, he picked it up and headed toward the deep black chair at the end of the aisle. Louisa pulled some mugs from behind the counter and motioned Mom to a stool.

Augie briefly wondered whether he should be relieved or worried.

Nestled in the chair, next to the photo of the white lady and black gentleman on their picnic, he turned to the front page. To his delight, a new picture greeted him. A beautiful fairy stared out of the page. She had fine wrinkles around her eyes and mouth, and her hair shone gold and silver. Her arm pointed straight out, and her wand stood poised for magic. Augie thrilled at her fierce look of determination.

THE
FAIRY GODMOTHER
TAKES CHARGE

T HE KING, PRINCESS ANNETTE'S FATHER, had been crazed. When he had seen his daughter in his gardens that fateful day, he had caught a vision of his long-lost wife. In the year and a half that followed, this vision never blurred. And when Annette fled with the donkey skin, it had been as if he had lost his queen all over again.

As he readied an onslaught of soldiers to ferret his daughter out, the princess's fairy godmother spoke up.

"Shame on you," she said. "You banish your daughter for fifteen years, then offer incest as a route to freedom. When she refuses this travesty, you intend to persecute her. What has she done to deserve this punishment?"

The king really looked at the fairy godmother, perhaps for the first time ever. He saw an ancient and strong figure, with burning eyes and a halo of gold and silver

47

hair. Her quiet voice echoed throughout his grand hall. Not a soul dared to speak.

The king raised his hand in anger, but words refused to cross his lips. He sat, frozen, watching the fairy, who calmly returned his gaze. Then, slowly, the king lowered his arm. Gathering his robes around him, as if to protect himself from a biting wind, he fled the throne room.

When he emerged from his chambers days later, he was haggard and repentant. He had faced his insanity and wrestled it to the ground. It would not rise again.

He called his advisers.

"Search for my daughter," he croaked. "I need to ask her for forgiveness."

And so they searched, for days, for weeks, for months, in vain. When the fairy godmother was satisfied that the king's heart was true, she asked for an audience.

"I can tell you where the princess hides," she said. "But please, Your Highness, leave her in peace. I will arrange a good match for her, and she will know happiness."

The king agreed.

When Princess Annette found her true love in Prince François, the king found peace as well.

"My kingdom shall be theirs when I die," he proclaimed.

And it was so.

A Visit to the Park

AUGIE LIKED HAPPY ENDINGS with good people coming to a good end. Too bad his life was filled with miserable beginnings. On Sunday morning, in Walter Jones's honor, Mom cleaned their tiny apartment—twice.

"You have to make the right impression," she said.

Augie didn't get it. No matter how clean the place was, they couldn't hide the old TV, the aluminum and Formica table, and the rickety mismatched chairs. It was what they had. A dull shine wasn't going to change it. The house never bothered Augie, but Mom fussed if anyone visited.

Augie briefly thought of sneaking down the back stairs, but he had agreed to this visit. Besides, Mom would freak—the gang several blocks down had been particularly rowdy last night, firing a gun at midnight. She had given Augie strict instructions not to leave the house today without an adult.

The doorbell rang. Mom clicked off the radio.

"Why don't you answer that while I put away the mop?" she said.

Augie moved slowly downstairs. He'd go through with this visit, but he hadn't promised to be friendly.

When Augie opened the front door, he noticed Dwaine Malloy across the street, sitting on a stoop near some crushed beer cans. He was eyeing Walter's truck. Augie could tell what Dwaine was thinking. No one was going to mistake this truck for a social worker's car. What was this big white dude doing here anyway?

Before Augie had a chance to grunt hello, Mom was there, extra lipstick gobbed on and her long hair let loose from its ponytail. She ushered Walter to the kitchen table, as if he were one of her customers at the diner, and offered him some iced tea. Her voice was too cheerful.

"I like to know who's spending time with my boy."

Augie cringed.

Mom mixed instant tea with water, and Walter accepted the glass with thanks. He swallowed the liquid in a few big gulps. Augie saw Mom's eyebrows rise slightly. At least she hadn't told the man to drink it slower, and Walter didn't seem to have noticed her disapproval. He placed the glass next to the sink.

"It's a nice day to visit Pear Hill Park," he said.

Mom nodded and smiled one of her better waitress smiles, the one she used for diners who tipped well. Now her voice was syrupy.

"That sounds lovely."

Why was she acting so weird? If Augie hadn't wanted to go anywhere with Walter before, he sure did now. Who knew how badly Mom was going to embarrass him if they hung around any longer?

"Let's go," he said.

Dwaine was still on the stoop when Walter unlocked the truck. Dwaine reminded Augie why he didn't want to have anything to do with the Big Brother program. It was for little kids. As soon as Dwaine figured out who Walter was, he'd tell Sergio and Fox Tooth and they'd have yet another reason to beat Augie up.

"Who's the kid checking us out?" Walter asked.

Augie sat low in the seat.

"Just someone from the neighborhood."

They drove awhile along a local highway, passing fast-food joints, gas stations, and discount stores.

"What can I tell you about myself?" Walter asked.

The question surprised Augie. Adults usually pestered *him* for information. "How do you like school?" "What are your hobbies?" "Who are your friends?" As if being grown-up meant that they were entitled to know everything about him. Over time, he had worked out a set of one- or two-word answers to put them off. "Okay." "Hanging out." "Some guys." The social worker from the Big Brother program had asked "follow-up" questions: "Does okay mean good or not so good?" "Where do you hang out?" "Could you give me some names?" Those had been a pain. Augie believed that the less she knew the better, and he had degenerated into grunts pretty quickly.

He hadn't thought about what he might want to know about a grown man. They drove past two sets of traffic lights while he pondered what to ask. Walter seemed patient, steering steadily in the center lane.

"Do you cut yourself a lot when you shave?" Augie said.

Walter smiled, like he approved of the question, then rubbed his chin with a hand. "Sometimes I do. It depends on what kind of razor I use, or if I use shaving cream."

Augie waited for more.

"I use disposable razors," Walter explained. "The older the razor, the duller the blade, and the more likely I am to scrape myself."

"Does it hurt?"

Walter shrugged. "Sometimes a little."

Augie understood. If it did, it didn't matter. That was the way it worked.

They entered a large park. It looked nothing like the dirty square down the street from Augie's house. Here were rolling paths, big trees, a lake with birds, even some clean pigeons. Walter took him to a concession stand and bought him a soda.

"They rent rowboats," Walter said. "Interested?"

Augie thought for a second. Truthfully, he didn't know. He'd never been on a boat before, and floating above deep water didn't have all that much appeal. But he didn't want Walter to think he was a wimp.

"Okay, I guess."

The life vest the attendant gave him proved uncomfortable. It was too large and pushed up under Augie's ears when he sat. Walter rowed them around. Augie decided he didn't like the tippy feeling at all, and he gripped the boat's metal edges. He didn't dare look around; his glasses had already begun slipping down his sweaty nose. Augie hated his clunky glasses, but he knew he couldn't afford to lose them in the lake. Mom had spent almost a week's tips to buy them in the first place.

"Would you like to see the other shore?" Walter asked.

Augie shook his head, carefully. Walter crumpled his chin.

"You look about as happy as a colt about to be gelded."

Augie had no idea what a colt about to be gelded might look like, but Walter had turned the boat around and was rowing back to the dock. Augie was relieved.

"It's okay to tell me my ideas stink," Walter said, mooring the boat.

They sat on the pier for a while. From this solid outpost, Augie kind of enjoyed watching the water lap up on the shore. The silver flecks in the ripples were mesmerizing. They must have done something to his brain, because he hadn't planned the next thing that came out of his mouth.

"I don't know how to swim."

Damn. He shook himself. What a stupid thing to say. Yet Walter wasn't laughing. He stared into the water.

"I learned late, too. It was one of the reasons kids beat me up."

"You got beat up?"

Augie had trouble imagining that. Walter looked so large and powerful. Who would try to hit him? But Walter scowled, remembering.

"I was the favorite punching bag."

"You're so big—why would kids go after you?"

"I wasn't always this big," Walter said.

Augie thought about that for a moment. "Were you as little as me?"

Walter looked him over and pursed his lips. "I was an average-sized kid," he said, "but I stuck out."

"Why?"

"I never got it right. When kids were playing with action figures, I decided to build a space station. When race cars were in, I spent time admiring the drivers. When we traded baseball cards, I chose the ones with the friendliest faces and ignored their averages."

Yeah, Augie thought. He stuck out.

"Do you still fight?" he asked.

"Naw. My mother put an end to it."

Augie couldn't picture that. His mom would never mix it up with the kids in his neighborhood. "Stay away from them" was her usual advice. Augie's disbelief must have been obvious.

"Would you like me to tell you how she did it?" Walter offered.

Augie hesitated for a split second, then shrugged. He was dying to know, but he wasn't ready to reveal that to Walter.

Walter didn't seem bothered by Augie's indifference. He stood and walked along the water's edge, picking up stones as he went. After he had gathered a bunch, he flipped one toward the water. It skipped six times!

"How'd you do that?" Augie asked.

Walter showed him. There was a motion to the wrist. And the rock had to be just the right shape on one side. The first couple of stones sank, but by the fourth throw, Augie got the stone to skip once. They worked at skipping stones for a while, until Walter said it was time to drive back.

"Your mom will be expecting us."

Mom behaved like her regular self when Augie got home. She gave him a real hug and her voice sounded normal. Even the extra lipstick was gone. She asked him how it had been.

"Okay," he answered.

He turned on the radio and began to hum. He didn't know whether he'd see Walter Jones again. But he did wonder how Walter's mother put an end to the fights.

"Rich Boy"

BEFORE SCHOOL MONDAY MORNING, Dwaine cornered Augie and demanded to know who Walter was.

"Just a friend," Augie said.

"Your *friend* has a nice truck."

Augie shrugged and tried to shy away. Dwaine shoved him hard against the wall.

"This is our turf. You get anything from the man, we want half."

Dwaine gave Augie an extra push before allowing him to escape.

That week, he spent every afternoon in Mr. Franklin's music room.

On Saturday, Dwaine was on the stoop again when Walter picked Augie up to go bowling. His mean little eyes glinted like broken glass.

"That kid means business," Walter said.

"Yeah," Augie replied.

They pulled away from the curb. Walter spent the next few blocks with his lips pursed.

"If he causes trouble, call me," he said.

Augie nodded but knew he wouldn't.

The real trouble started soon after. Like almost everyone else in school, Augie paid a reduced lunch rate, but Mom sometimes gave him a little extra to save up for a treat. He almost never spent it in the cafeteria—he'd store the change in the box behind the couch at home, until he had enough to buy a comic book or some candy at the bodega. One day, Dwaine must have seen him put the extra quarter back into his pocket. Before Augie made it to the playground door, Dwaine had him pinned to a locker. Sergio and Fox Tooth closed in.

"I see you have some extra cash," Dwaine said.

"From the truck man?" Sergio said.

Dwaine had told them about Walter. Augie wasn't surprised.

"It's mine," Augie said.

Dwaine's grip tightened. Sergio stepped close.

"Rich boys share their wealth."

Augie couldn't believe it. All he had was a quarter,

and they wanted it. He tried to struggle. Dwaine smacked him upside the head. Augie saw stars as pain shot through his temple. His glasses were knocked sideways.

"Hand it over," Dwaine said.

"Now, Perfessor," Sergio said. "No point arguing 'bout this."

Augie's head throbbed. Twenty-five cents wasn't worth getting beat up over. Augie nodded and reached into his pocket for the coin. He felt tears prickling in his eyes. He wouldn't cry! Especially not in front of these guys. He swallowed, then croaked, "Here."

"What's going on?"

Mr. Franklin stood over the boys. Dwaine let go. The quarter fell to the floor.

"Dwaine Malloy?" Mr. Franklin said.

His voice was low, cold as ice. Dwaine seemed to be turning green.

"Just a misunderstanding, sir," Sergio said. "It's been worked out already."

Mr. Franklin looked at the four of them, incredulous.

"Mr. Boretski, please come with me."

What had Augie done wrong? He had been rescued, but now he was in trouble with Mr. Franklin. As soon as the large teacher turned around, Fox Tooth swiped the quarter off the floor and grinned. Miserable, Augie followed Mr. Franklin to the classroom.

"I had some notion, Mr. Boretski, that you were a bit more serious than that crowd."

Did Mr. Franklin believe Augie wanted to be with them? That was crazy. But Augie wasn't going to talk back. He knew that would just get him into deeper trouble. He kept his gaze to the floor, hoping the pain in the side of his head would fade.

"Perhaps you need to be kept busier," Mr. Franklin continued.

Augie looked up in fear. What did Mr. Franklin have in mind? The man had one hand on a stack of papers on his desk, the other on a stapler.

"This'll go faster if I have some help."

Mr. Franklin handed Augie the stack. Augie breathed a sigh of relief—he wasn't being punished. He glanced down at the papers. Printed in large bold letters was the following:

AUDITIONS FOR JUNIOR CHORUS
MONDAY, OCTOBER 1
3 p.m.–5 p.m.
CAFETERIA STAGE
ALL VOICE PARTS NEEDED
QUESTIONS MAY BE ADDRESSED TO MR. FRANKLIN

For the next fifteen minutes, Augie followed Mr. Franklin around the school, handing him one flyer at a time. Mr. Franklin stapled the announcements to bulletin boards. When the bell rang, only one flyer was left.

"You may keep it," Mr. Franklin said.

Dwaine, Sergio, and Fox Tooth smiled at Augie when he entered the classroom. He knew they weren't being friendly. The next morning, they were waiting for him at the classroom door.

"Well, now, look who's here," Sergio called.

"Rich Boy," Dwaine chortled.

Fox Tooth grinned. Augie didn't like the sound of his new nickname. What were they planning now?

He found out at noon. After a boring morning of math drills and history, Augie was ready for lunch. He shouldn't have put away his notebook after class, because that gave Fox Tooth the chance to get out of the classroom first. Augie was halfway to the cafeteria when Fox Tooth stepped in front of him.

"Time to share the wealth," he said.

Dwaine and Sergio had caught up. Augie was surrounded. He had no choice. He handed over his lunch money.

"Now there's a good Rich Boy," Sergio laughed as the three boys headed toward the cafeteria.

The following day, Augie made sure he was out the door and into the cafeteria first. But afterward they cornered him in the playground.

"Cough up," Dwaine said.

"Don't got nothin'," Augie said.

Augie never saw the punch, but he felt Dwaine's fist as it landed in his stomach. As he fell to the ground, Fox Tooth shielded them from the playground monitor's view.

"Now, Rich Boy," Sergio said, "don't you *ever* forget our cut."

Either they beat him, or Augie wound up hungry. Getting desperate, he asked his mom if he could pack his lunch instead. She seemed surprised but agreed.

"I'll get you the ingredients," she said, "but you'll have to make it."

On Monday, he brought a peanut butter sandwich to school with some carrot sticks. He didn't rush from the classroom at the lunch bell. Dwaine, Sergio, and Fox Tooth were waiting for him in the hall.

"Where's our money?" Dwaine demanded.

"Don't have any," Augie said.

Sergio snatched the bag from him.

"Well, right thoughtful of you," Sergio said. "He brought us food."

The boys walked away, leaving Augie empty-handed again.

It wasn't fair! He kicked the nearest locker in misery, but his stomach rumbled louder. No way was he going to walk into the cafeteria and watch them eat his lunch. He ran down the steps to the music room. The lights were off. Good. That meant Mr. Franklin wasn't there. Augie sat in a corner behind some chairs, his back to one of the heating vents, and put his head on his knees.

He must have fallen asleep because he was jolted awake when the lights came on. He couldn't see very well with the chairs in front of him, but he recognized Mr. Franklin's pants and shoes and the peculiar lumber in his walk. He heard a paper bag being unrolled and the snap of Mr. Franklin's briefcase being opened. Mr. Franklin was having lunch while doing some work, Augie guessed.

Augie sat very still, because he didn't want to be caught. Not moving was harder than he expected. Probably no more than fifteen minutes had passed, but to Augie, the wait felt like hours.

Then he heard the rustle of papers, the scrape of Mr. Franklin's chair, the snap of the briefcase closing. Augie saw Mr. Franklin's legs come around the front of the desk and walk straight in his direction. Oh no, he had been seen! He ducked his head down and covered it with his hands.

Mr. Franklin stopped and cleared his throat. Augie almost jumped out of his skin, but he didn't dare look up. There was a crumple of paper, a thunk, and

Mr. Franklin retreated. Mr. Franklin scooped up his briefcase, turned the lights off, and walked out the door. Augie peeked up. He hadn't noticed the trash can a few feet away.

His back hurt him some when he straightened, and his legs didn't seem to want to unbend. But he managed to get up. The lunch period must be almost over, he thought. He snuck toward the door.

"You goin' to try out?"

Augie heard Dwaine's voice on the other side of the door. He scrambled behind the desk.

"Maybe," Sergio answered. "Dunno."

Augie recognized Fox Tooth's weird giggle.

"You think it's funny?" Sergio asked.

His tone sounded threatening. Augie figured Fox Tooth must have cowered and had probably shaken his head, because Sergio spoke again with authority.

"The only question is: Do I get the right treatment? I'm the star. Slammin', jammin' Sergio. Don't you see the lights?"

"Not if Mr. Franklin's in charge," Dwaine said.

"Who cares?" Sergio replied. "I'll stand out no matter what, and I'll have girls wantin' a piece of my shirt."

Augie almost didn't hear that last part because they were walking away. He stood. The light from the hallway shone through the window at the top of the door, leaving a bright square on the desk. Augie blinked.

There was an apple. Mr. Franklin must have left it. Augie hesitated, but only for a second. Mr. Franklin wasn't coming back. He had turned off the light. Augie managed to wolf down most of the fruit before the bell rang.

From Bad to Worse

MOM FOUND THE FLYER while cleaning up.

"So you're going to audition?"

Augie shrugged. No, he thought, he wasn't, especially after he had overheard Sergio's plan. The last thing Augie wanted was to be in a chorus with someone whom he spent all of his energy trying to avoid.

"You really should," Mom persisted. "You have a good voice."

Augie buried his nose in his history book.

"I have a test tomorrow," he said.

The auditions weren't for two weeks, but the school was already abuzz. No one could remember the last time there had been an after-school activity of any sort.

And the prospect of a show had everyone excited. Even Mr. Smith, the school custodian, had taken the time to dust off the old piano, although Augie doubted Mr. Franklin was going to use it. The last time some kid had played on the keys, it had sounded all out of tune. Walking down the hallways, he passed kids singing snatches of songs. Some even posed in front of friends for effect. Augie thought they were pretty funny.

Augie loved to sing. But to him it was like breathing. He did it because he couldn't help himself. He hummed along with the radio without ever thinking about it. And on the rare evening when his mom wasn't working and she wasn't bone-tired, and there was nothing good on TV and nothing else to do in the house, the two of them sang old tunes she had taught him. He thought they sounded nice together.

Mom didn't pester him about the audition, though. By Saturday, Augie figured she had forgotten about it. He watched cartoons all morning in peace, and Walter took him to the aquarium afterward. What a cool place, with sharks and all. He spent a chunk of Sunday morning telling Mom about it. "My, you have a lot to say," she said. But she was smiling, and she whistled as she got ready for work.

By late afternoon, Mom had laid out his supper. He sat at the table while she gathered her keys. They heard Mrs. Lorentushki's daughter pick her up for Sunday dinner. Mom pecked Augie on the cheek.

"Don't forget the trash when you're done," she said.

He finished off the macaroni and cheese, washed the plate, and headed downstairs, plastic bag in hand. The narrow alley where they kept the cans was dark. Augie had just dropped the bag into one of the containers when he was grabbed from behind and spun around. Dwaine's face was so close, Augie could count each of his eyelashes. Dwaine twisted Augie's collar into his fists.

"So, Augustus, what'd the man give you?"

Out of the corner of his eye, Augie saw Sergio and Fox Tooth, waiting. Augie tried to swallow but couldn't.

"Looks like he ain't talkin'," said Sergio.

Fox Tooth grinned.

"Now ain't that too bad."

Dwaine tightened a fist. Augie could feel the knuckles dig into his windpipe.

"I told you half."

"I don't have anything," Augie squeaked.

Dwaine lifted Augie up like a sack.

"Drop him," Sergio ordered.

Even before Augie hit the ground, Fox Tooth had started kicking. Augie curled up tight into a ball, but Fox Tooth only kicked harder around his shoulders and head. One of the kicks grazed an ear and knocked his glasses clear down the alley. He swallowed a scream; it felt as if his ear had been ripped off.

"Next time, you have something," Sergio hissed, "or we'll check out your insides."

Fox Tooth gave one last kick to Augie's bruised legs, and the three of them walked away as if nothing had happened.

A long time passed before Augie managed to stand. Every bit of him hurt. He took even more time to find his glasses in the dark alleyway. Miraculously, the frames were intact, although one of the lenses had cracked. Slowly, very slowly, Augie limped up the back stairs and sat at the edge of the couch. He didn't move until the apartment was dark.

When he did get up, he hurt so bad he almost fell down.

What was he going to do? He couldn't call his mother. She'd panic and zoom him over to the emergency room and lose a night's pay. They couldn't afford that.

This whole problem was Walter's fault. If he hadn't shown up, none of this would have happened. Dwaine, Sergio, and Fox Tooth seemed to think Augie was getting presents from him.

He heard a car pull up and one of its doors slam.

"I'll call tomorrow," a woman said.

"You take care of my grandchildren," Mrs. Lorentushki replied.

The door downstairs creaked open and clicked shut as Mrs. Lorentushki entered her apartment. The car drove away.

Maybe Mrs. Lorentushki could help? Augie pushed

the thought away. That old woman? She'd panic worse than Mom.

He flipped on the fluorescent light. The glare stung his eyes. He cursed Walter. He had gotten Augie into this trouble. He had better well get him out of it. Where had Mom put his number?

Only after he heard the phone ring on the other end did Augie wonder whether he really wanted Walter to be home.

"Yes?" a man answered.

It wasn't Walter. Augie's first instinct was to hang up, but he was sure he had dialed the right number.

"Could I speak with Walter Jones?"

He heard the phone being put down, laughter in the background, and the sound of a chair scraping the floor.

"Hello?" Walter said.

"It's Augie."

Silence. Was Walter angry that Augie had interrupted him when he had guests?

"What's up?"

The tone wasn't annoyed. Okay, Augie thought, he could go through with this.

"I need to speak to you."

"I'm all ears."

This was going to be harder than Augie thought. He should have told Mom that he didn't want a Big Brother anymore, and that would have been the end of it. He'd been stupid calling this guy.

"I'll talk to you another time," Augie said.

He had almost hung up when he heard Walter's call from the receiver: "Wait!"

Augie put the phone back to his ear.

"Are you in trouble?" Walter asked.

Augie didn't reply. The silence dragged for several seconds.

"Still there?" Walter said.

"Uh-huh."

"I'll be right over."

After Augie hung up the phone, he switched off the light and crumpled onto the recliner. He began to sob.

To the Rescue

AUGIE HEARD WALTER'S TRUCK pull up in front of the house. He looked out the window. Walter was talking to someone inside the cab as he locked it up. Who did Walter bring? Damn. Augie shouldn't have called him.

He heard Mrs. Lorentushki's voice at the front door.

"Mr. Jones. Why are you here?"

He didn't hear Walter's reply, but she let him in.

"He's not upstairs," Mrs. Lorentushki said. "No radio today."

"May I give their door a knock?"

Augie heard Walter climb the stairs.

"Augie, it's Walter."

Augie cracked the door open.

"May I come in?" Walter asked.

"Come down if you need something," Mrs. Lorentushki called.

Augie opened the door wider and allowed Walter into the living room.

"Mind if I turn this on?" Walter said, reaching for a lamp.

The light blinded Augie. When his eyesight adjusted, he saw Walter's shocked expression. He glanced at his distorted reflection in the TV: the left side of his face was swollen, his glasses were cracked, and he had smeared blood from his hands onto his forehead.

"Who did this?" Walter demanded. Walter's arm muscles bulged. He clenched his fists.

Augie shook his head. "You report them, they'll go after me worse," he said.

Walter put a hand out to help Augie sit down. "Who's your doctor?" he asked.

"Don't have one," Augie replied.

Walter took a step toward the phone. "We'd better call your mom."

"*No!*" Augie yelled. Not his mother. What was the point of having Walter here if he was just going to call Mom?

Walter froze.

"No," Augie repeated. A sob caught his throat.

Walter sat down next to him, not letting the springs

bounce. The large man leaned his elbows on his knees and stared at the darkened television in the corner.

"She's going to find out eventually," he said.

"Not if I get cleaned up first."

"And what if they broke something?"

"We'll get it patched up without her. She doesn't have to know."

Walter shook his head. "Only your mom can authorize medical care," he said. "I'm not your father."

"Who said anything about you being my father?"

Augie had jumped up. Pain shot up his legs.

"You got me into this!" he yelled. "You get me out."

Walter appeared shocked. At that moment they were interrupted by a series of loud barks followed by a spine-tingling howl.

"That's Jesse," Walter said as he sprang toward the door. "Be right back."

Augie looked out the front window. Sergio, Fox Tooth, and Dwaine crouched by the side of Walter's pickup. A large dog was leaping at the windows inside the truck. That must be Jesse, Augie thought. They clearly hadn't expected this.

"Down, boy," Walter yelled as he raced out.

The kids scattered. Jesse kept on barking. The next thing Augie saw was Mrs. Lorentushki wielding a baseball bat and screaming after the receding figures.

"Punks! You stay away! I call the police!"

The next half hour passed in a fog. Mrs. Lorentushki walked Augie down to her apartment while Walter brought his old greyhound to her kitchen. She gave the dog a big bowl of water. Augie sat on a chair eyeing the dog nervously while she washed all of his scratches and scuffs and told Walter a long story about the puppy she had raised as a girl in Poland. She handed Augie an ice pack for his face.

"This will do," she said.

Walter, sitting in one of her upholstered armchairs, somehow seemed too big for her neat apartment.

"Shouldn't we call the police?" he said.

Mrs. Lorentushki shook her head. "All they do is file a report. If you call, the report is lost."

Augie knew she was right. Mrs. Lorentushki fluffed up a pillow and brought in a set of sheets.

"Now, you stay here," she told Augie. "When Mr. Jones leaves, we phone Mama."

No, Augie thought. But Mrs. Lorentushki wasn't going to give in on this one, he could tell. At least Augie didn't look quite so bad. He nodded. Then Augie noticed Walter. The man was shaking his head with a wry smile on his face.

The scene didn't feel right to Augie, with Mrs. Lorentushki fussing at the couch, Walter in the armchair, and the dog under the kitchen table. None of it was right. And for all he knew, Dwaine, Sergio, and Fox

Tooth might still be outside, lurking. He needed something to take his mind off of all this.

"Can I get something upstairs?" he asked.

"Of course," Mrs. Lorentushki said. "Mr. Jones, you go with."

Hobbling upstairs took him longer than he expected, and he needed Walter's help to pull out the couch so he could reach the book. Mom had agreed to keep it there—it was too precious to be left lying about.

"I didn't know you like to read," Walter said.

Augie looked at the green cover. "Not much," he said. He paused. "This is special."

Stupid mouth, working without his brain fully engaged. Naturally, that sparked Walter's interest.

"May I see?"

Augie hesitated before handing him the book. Walter turned it in his hands and read the engraved cover. He raised an eyebrow. Augie looked down at his shoes with his one good eye. He shouldn't have fetched the book—Walter thought he was dumb for reading it. He heard the gentle rustle of pages as Walter opened the volume.

"Nice illustration," Walter said.

Augie looked up. Walter showed him the front page. An elegant woman in flowing robes held a box over a pool of water. Trees, flowers, and vines surrounded her. Shadows and greens filled the page. The water twinkled black. The woman held her eyes closed while the box shone. What was this? Augie wondered.

"I can see why you like it," Walter added. He was referring to the book, which he had closed and was handing over.

"You know it?" Augie managed to ask.

Walter shook his head. "Just the author," he said.

Augie wondered what else Louisa Nordritch had written.

TO BUILD A
WOODEN BOX

O N A BEAUTIFUL DAY LONG ago, the fairy Louisa, still young and vigorous, journeyed to woods far away where people never came and were never welcome.

By a pond whose depth no one could fathom, she found a felled tree, aged by time and the magical air into a hard log. She inspected it carefully. No animal used it as a home. Moss grew at one end. It was abandoned, she felt sure. With a stone saw (for fairies are no friends of metal), she cut even lengths.

Along the edges of the pool she found cast-off stones to use as rivets, and shells to use as hinges. She hammered and fashioned, and a small wooden box took shape.

From her pocket she pulled out a large, perfect pearl. She whispered into her hand.

"In exchange for your gifts."

Then she threw the globe into the water. With the box, she caught the droplets from the splash.

From another pocket she took a vial filled with honey, which she poured into a wide stone plate. She set the plate on a tree stump and soon bees came. Over the course of two days, the bees consumed the honey. Huddled in her cloak, the fairy Louisa watched and waited. By the dawn of the third day, all of the honey was gone. With a fine linen cloth, never before used, Louisa wiped the plate, over and over, until it shone clean. Then with this same cloth, she began polishing her box, imparting every little bit of wax and pollen from the bees into the wood. This took another day.

Louisa was weary. But her work was almost done.

She dug out from her cloak shimmering silks, intricate lace, a ruby, a diamond, and a sapphire. She opened her small box and laid these riches across the opening. Then she ate some hard cheese, drank a flask of wine, and allowed herself to sleep.

When Louisa awoke, the box was where she had left it, but the gifts were gone. The lid was shut, and across the top lay a garland of daisies.

The fairy Louisa smiled. The masters of the forest had approved of her work and had allowed her to keep it. With care, she lifted her magic box.

Stomachaches and Other Truths

WHAT I NEED, AUGIE thought, *is a fairy godmother. She'd wave her magic wand, and* poof, *all my problems would disappear.*

But nothing seemed to make his tormentors disappear. Although Augie's body was healing and his glasses were fixed, Dwaine, Sergio, and Fox Tooth dogged him wherever he went. His only refuge during the day was their classroom. The class didn't mess with Mr. Franklin.

When Friday rolled around and a sub showed up instead of Mr. Franklin, bedlam broke loose. With the paper airplanes, constant talking, and nonsense responses to questions, the substitute teacher was close to tears by the lunch bell. Everyone was so riled up, Augie figured he'd best spend all of lunch in the music room to be safe. But he found the music room locked—Mr. Franklin wasn't around to open it!

Augie ran to the nurse's office and faked a stomach-ache. He doubled over so convincingly that the nurse called Mom to pick him up. Mom missed work that night to stay home with him. Augie had never felt so guilty.

Saturday morning she sat at the foot of his sofa bed. "How's the stomach?" she asked.

"Fine," he said.

The answer might have been true, but he wasn't feeling fine. He felt awful lying to Mom.

"Do you think you'll be up for a visit from Walter?" she said.

"Sure."

Augie started to get out of bed.

"I called and told him you were sick yesterday. He said he'd come for a short visit and then let you recuperate."

Augie sank back onto his pillow. He had begun to look forward to his afternoons out with Walter. Well, he supposed, he deserved to be stuck in here.

"And that way," Mom continued, "I'll get to know him better."

Oh no.

Even if Mom didn't embarrass him this time, he wasn't eager to have Walter spend time with her. Her tight jeans and T-shirts might look nice, but Augie wondered whether mothers were supposed to dress that way. And what if she flirted with Walter? Augie'd die.

Mom helped Augie turn his bedroom back into the living room.

"I'll get us some snacks," she said.

Grabbing her purse, she headed out the door.

Walter arrived early.

"Mom'll be back soon," Augie explained. "She went to the bodega."

Walter nodded. "I heard you were under the weather."

Augie didn't want to talk about how he was feeling, so he shrugged. Walter lowered his large frame into the recliner. There were a few minutes of awkward silence, filled only by some songs from an oldies station Mom had tuned to.

"I like the music," Walter said.

Augie thought it was okay, but not his favorite. "Mom's taste."

Walter smiled like he had been caught doing something he wasn't supposed to. This annoyed Augie. Mom walked in at that moment, holding a grocery bag with one hand while she wrestled the keys out of the door with the other. Walter jumped up and took the bag from her, setting it on the kitchen table.

"I didn't expect such a long line at the market," she said.

For the next few minutes, Augie's mom and Walter

bustled in the small kitchen that opened into the living room. Walter was handy, Augie realized. He knew what stuff needed to go in the fridge, and he helped set out some cookies next to the couch. He looked comfortable in their house.

For a split second Augie wondered if Mom thought so, too. A wave of confusion hit him. He didn't want Walter to feel comfortable with his mom.

Augie's father had disappeared before Augie turned two. Mom had told the story often enough. She and Howie Boretski were sixteen when Augie was born. They quit high school to get married, and Howie took a job at the soup factory. But the factory closed. According to Mom, jobs were scarce, so Howie gave up looking and headed west.

"Didn't he love you?" Augie used to ask.

"Howie and I were too young," Mom always answered.

Her answer never made any sense. Augie was young, and *he* knew how to love his mom.

Augie didn't remember his father. Mom kept a picture in the night table—an old snapshot in a brown metal frame. It must have been taken at a carnival. Howie was holding cotton candy and Mom looked tired but happy, carrying Augie with a pacifier in his mouth. That was really embarrassing, so Augie was glad the picture wasn't out for everyone to see. But sometimes, when Mom wasn't around, he'd sneak it out and look at his father's round face, blue eyes, and curly brown hair. Augie had inherited Mom's brown eyes and straight hair, and he wondered whether his father would recognize him if he ever saw him.

Augie had always wanted to meet his dad. With his dad around, Mom wouldn't have signed him up with the Big Brother program, and he wouldn't have these problems with Dwaine, Sergio, and Fox Tooth. Instead, he was stuck with Walter.

Boring Walter, Augie added to himself. The man had spent the last five minutes describing his business to Mom. ("The market for organic vegetables is growing.") Bo-ring.

Augie nibbled on the dry toast Mom had insisted he eat.

"It's funny," Mom was saying to Walter, "if this was the first time I met you, I'd have never guessed you owned a greenhouse."

Augie winced. Leave it to Mom to say something truly embarrassing.

Walter laughed. "Didn't expect it myself," he said.

"Oh?"

"A friend convinced me," he said. "See, I was living in Philadelphia and was miserable."

Walter had lived in Philly? Augie started to pay attention.

"My friend owns a bookstore, and she showed me a bunch of books on horticulture."

Augie sat forward.

"Why horticulture?" Mom asked.

"I'm not sure," Walter said. "Louisa's the kind of person who can see into people's souls."

Mom was nodding at this mushy stuff. Augie was riveted by the name. Louisa.

"I grew up on a farm," Walter continued. "We raised horses, mostly."

"Sounds nice," Mom said.

"It was okay, I guess." Walter ran a hand through his hair. "I left it planning never to return. When I saw those books, I turned Louisa down. I told her, 'I came to Philly to find a new center.' "

"What did she say?" Mom asked.

" 'Your center is within you.' "

Mom nodded again.

"I read them, you know," Walter said, "and I couldn't get enough of them. I found a love of farming I had buried when I had left my parents' farm. And when the greenhouse went up for sale, I jumped at it."

Mom passed him the plate of cookies. "Sounds like you did the right thing."

Walter seemed so relaxed. His eyes crinkled, even when he wasn't smiling. Why did this bother Augie?

"Mrs. Lorentushki tells me you have a greyhound," Mom continued. "Where does he stay during the day?"

"He's not mine," Walter said. "Jesse belongs to Roger."

Mom seemed satisfied by the answer and brought

the empty plate to the sink. Augie, however, was curious. "Who's Roger?"

"My partner," Walter replied.

Oh, Augie thought, someone he worked with.

Soon after, Walter left. Augie grumbled while they straightened up.

"Walter didn't tell you where they keep Jesse."

Mom shrugged.

"Roger Hoover owns a lot of land. The dog probably has a run behind his business."

Augie thought about this for a minute.

"How do you know Roger Hoover?" he finally asked.

Mom placed the last glass onto the dish rack and dried her hands.

"I serve him lunch almost every day."

"I thought he worked on the other side of town, with Walter."

Mom smiled.

"No, hon. He owns the Pear Hill Hardware Store."

Mom saw Augie's confusion.

"Roger and Walter live together."

They live together? They're partners? They're a couple! Augie had trouble believing it. He was spending time with a gay man.

"Does Mrs. Lorentushki know?" Augie was thinking about how she had invited Walter into her living room.

"I don't know for sure. Maybe," Mom said.

Augie felt a squeeze in his stomach.

He knew what happened to gay kids. Lebron Travis, a boy who had been in sixth grade two years ago, was gay—at least everyone said he was. Even in fourth grade, Augie knew to stay away from him—Lebron was the biggest, most visible target in school. On Halloween, Lebron had worn a dress. A week later, Lebron was gone. Augie never saw him in school again. Rumor had it that they had found him in the square near Augie's house, cut up real bad, nearly dead.

Augie sat on the couch while Mom began sorting dirty clothes for the Laundromat. He knew he should help, but the squeeze in his stomach had only gotten worse. Mom knew Walter was gay, and she let him take Augie on outings. What if Dwaine figured it out?

Augie crossed his arms, clutching his sides in fear. Mom looked up.

"Sweetie, you look pale." She frowned and put her hand on his forehead. "Let's pull out the bed. You rest today."

Augie didn't protest. He wouldn't be safe anywhere else.

Cutting Losses

AUGIE PLANNED IT CAREFULLY. He waited until Mom had left for work. Then he waited a little longer, until Mrs. Lorentushki's daughter picked her up for Sunday dinner. He rehearsed the words over and over in his head: *Walter, it's me, Augie. Thanks for being my Big Brother and all the stuff you've done with me, but I think that I'm really too old for a Big Brother. Maybe the program can set you up with a younger kid.*

He sat in front of the phone, willing himself to dial. But his hands didn't move. This was tougher than he had expected.

It wasn't fair. He had started liking Walter. Walter

never pushed. Walter didn't make demands. Walter was reliable. And sometimes Augie really had fun.

Except for being beat up, he reminded himself. That was Walter's fault.

But he knew that wasn't entirely true, either.

Why were things so difficult?

Having a Big Brother, like some little kid, was bad enough, but this Big Brother was gay! What if Dwaine or Sergio or Fox Tooth found out? They'd think Augie was gay, too, and he'd be lucky if he survived what they'd do to him then. Augie had to put an end to this.

He took a deep breath and picked up the phone. A man answered on the second ring.

"Hello?"

The voice wasn't Walter's. It must be that Roger Hoover person. This really wasn't going to be easy.

"Could I please speak with Walter Jones?"

"Sure. Are you Augie?" The man sounded pleased.

"Uh. Yeah. Could I speak with Walter?"

"Of course."

Augie heard Roger Hoover call Walter to the phone.

"You okay?" Walter asked as soon as he got on the line.

Augie hadn't expected that. The question threw him for a second. But he was determined to go through with this.

"I'm fine, it's just that I have something important to ask you."

"Sure. Anything you want."

That wasn't what Walter was supposed to say. Why was he being so nice?

"It's about the Big Brother thing," Augie began. "I'm not sure if I'm happy with it. You see . . ." He let the words trail. He had lost track of what he was going to say. There were a few seconds of silence while Augie tried to recapture what he had planned, but Walter jumped in.

"I'm sorry, Augie. I know those kids have been tough on you."

"That's not it." Walter was screwing this up. How had Augie planned it, now? He desperately tried to recall the words he had rehearsed, but they refused to come back. He'd have to improvise.

"It's just, well, I'm not sure I want a Big Brother."

"Oh."

Augie heard Walter's disappointment in that small "oh." Or was it hurt?

"Can you tell me why?" Walter asked. His voice was gentle.

"It's for little kids. I'm too old to start. Gotta go. It's getting late."

Augie had said it very fast, and when he hung up, he stared at the phone for a long time. He half hoped that it would ring, that Walter would be on the other end of the line, that he would beg Augie to change his mind. But the phone remained silent.

This had been what Augie wanted, he reasoned. This was his way out with the guys. With no Walter around, they wouldn't hound him for money. No one would beat him up for being some gay guy's friend. No one would think he was gay, either. In time, Walter Jones would be forgotten, and Augie's life would return to what it had been before.

To what it had been before. No friend. No weekends to look forward to.

In the silence, Augie felt worse and worse.

Auditions

MOM HADN'T BOUGHT IT, not for a second.

"You liked Walter. You had fun with him. What happened?"

"Nothing," Augie replied. "I told you I didn't want a Big Brother."

"But you guys clicked," Mom insisted.

"Leave me alone," Augie said.

He stuffed his lunch into his pack and stalked out of the apartment. He pulled it out on his way to school, eating it to avoid having it stolen at lunchtime. He knew that by the afternoon, he would be hungry, but there was always Mrs. Lorentushki's snack to look forward to.

At the end of the day, he saw Dwaine and Fox Tooth

huddled near the front door. He headed for the music room, his stomach pinched, figuring he'd only have to wait a few minutes and then he'd leave. But then Mr. Franklin showed up.

"Augustus," he said. "I'm glad I ran into you. I could use help with the auditions."

Augie had forgotten all about them! Mr. Franklin took a clipboard out of the desk and handed it to Augie. Augie looked at it. The names of all the kids who had signed up were listed on two sheets of paper.

Augie had to run to keep up with Mr. Franklin, who strode to the cafeteria with giant steps, a huge box of crackers under one arm, his briefcase under the other.

"What do you want me to do?" Augie asked.

"Read off the names, of course," Mr. Franklin said.

The cafeteria was full. Augie counted more than fifty kids on the list, but even more than that were milling around. They must have come to watch the show, or make fun of it. He wasn't sure.

Mr. Franklin left the crackers by the door, causing a brief pileup as kids grabbed them from the box. Augie managed to get a few, quieting the worst of his stomach rumblings, then caught up with Mr. Franklin at the front of the room. Mr. Franklin pulled out from his briefcase a second clipboard with a complicated chart attached. Augie wondered what all the symbols meant.

Mr. Franklin cleared his throat, and quiet descended on the crowd.

"Fifty-eight students are auditioning," he said. "I will take anyone who can sing in tune and is willing to work. My goal today is to place your voice and your range."

Augie wasn't sure what Mr. Franklin meant, but he didn't explain any further.

"We have limited time, so, please, when your name is called, go up on the stage without fanfare. Give the name of the song you will sing, sing it, and step down."

All the kids nodded. A few snickers escaped from the crowd.

"Also," Mr. Franklin continued, "there will be no cheering, no booing, no noise whatsoever from on-lookers."

Silence.

"Is that understood?"

A sea of heads nodded with scattered murmurs of, "Yes, Mr. Franklin."

"Then let's begin."

Mr. Franklin looked down at Augie, who, after a second's hesitation, read the first name off the list.

"Annie Zola."

A girl in fourth grade stepped up. She had obviously spent some time thinking about what she was going to wear. Her T-shirt and pants were so clean they looked new. She probably bleached her sneakers, Augie thought. She wore colorful beads in her hair.

"Is it okay if I sing something from church?" she asked.

Someone in the back laughed. Augie was pretty sure he recognized Sergio's guffaw. Mr. Franklin gave that corner a dark look, and the laugh cut short.

"Of course, Annie," Mr. Franklin said. "Please begin."

In a slightly quavery voice, she sang a hymn. All the while Mr. Franklin took notes. Augie noticed his marks—arrows, circles, pluses, and minuses lined up in spaces in the grid. It didn't make much sense to Augie. When she finished, Mr. Franklin nodded.

"Very good. Thank you, Annie. You may step down."

"Fred Washington," Augie read.

A big, overweight boy in Augie's class stepped up. No snickers this time. He sang a Christmas carol.

"Very good," said Mr. Franklin. "Thank you. You may step down."

One after another, kids' names were called, they climbed the stage, they sang, Mr. Franklin thanked them, and they stepped down. The songs and voices merged after a while. How did Mr. Franklin tell them apart? Sure, there were the few who belted it out, and a bunch who sang everything flat, but most were somewhere in between—carrying a tune but not always with strength and not always on key. The whole while, Mr.

Franklin took notes, and the grids filled with names and symbols.

About halfway down the list, Augie came to the one name he had been dreading.

"Sergio Barnaby."

Sergio ambled up. He was carrying a boom box, which he set at his feet on the stage.

"This is my own song," Sergio announced. "I call it 'Sergio's Song.' "

Titters ran through the crowd. To Sergio's credit, he ignored them. He leaned over to press a button, but Mr. Franklin interrupted him.

"No accompaniment, Mr. Barnaby."

"But I need my bass line," Sergio protested.

Mr. Franklin shook his head. "No accompaniment."

Sergio looked at Mr. Franklin for a second but must have figured argument was futile. He lifted a knee, stomped his foot down, jutted his shoulder forward, and stared into the crowd. He began a hip-hop rant.

There was no way around it. The words were lame.

"I'm Sergio / I can fly / Watch me reach into the sky / Bring down everythin' up high. . . ."

Mr. Franklin's pen stood still for the first time all afternoon. But then Sergio launched into his chorus of jets, and nets, and bets, and a song emerged. It was tuneful. It had rhythm. And Sergio's voice wasn't bad, not bad at all. Mr. Franklin began writing.

When Sergio was done, he took a sweeping bow.

Mr. Franklin raked his gaze across the crowd, silencing any claps.

"Very good," he said. "Thank you. You may step down."

After Sergio's performance, the rest of the auditions dragged. By the time they reached the last few kids, the cafeteria was almost empty. Most had become bored and left. When the last girl finished the twelfth rendition of "Rudolph the Red-Nosed Reindeer," even Mr. Franklin looked tired.

"Very good," he said. "Thank you. You may step down."

She ran out to a woman who had been waiting in the doorway. Augie figured the woman was the girl's mom.

"Thank you, Augustus," Mr. Franklin said.

Augie returned the clipboard. Mr. Franklin stuffed it into his briefcase with his chart, then glanced at his watch.

"It's late. Do you have a ride home?"

Augie shook his head. He knew that the streets between the school and his home only became more dangerous as the afternoon slipped into evening. He hadn't planned on staying this late.

Mr. Franklin frowned. "I'll take you, then."

Augie ran down to the music room to get his things, and Mr. Franklin followed with the key. Augie scooped up his bag and grabbed his jacket.

"Your name wasn't on the list," Mr. Franklin said.

Augie shrugged.

"You don't like to sing?"

Mr. Franklin's voice had never struck Augie as friendly. But the tone this time seemed so open, Augie had to look him in the eyes. He couldn't lie to the man.

"I guess I do."

"I have a few more minutes," Mr. Franklin said. "Why don't you sing for me now?"

Augie was tired, and his hunger had returned. He had heard so many kids sing so many songs, so many of them the same. When he sang with his mom, he did it because it was fun, not because he had to.

He looked at the school bag that he had let drop to his feet and the jacket that he still held in his hands, and he thought of the last time he and Mom had sung together. Sometime back in March, a big snowstorm had struck the East Coast, and the power had gone out. Mrs. Lorentushki had asked Augie and his mom to come down to her place.

"I don't like it to be alone when it's so dark," she had explained.

They had lit a half dozen candles in Mrs. Lorentushki's living room, but the old woman still seemed nervous. She usually didn't scare so easy, so she had Augie worried. Then Mom had started singing some old songs she had learned when she was a teenager, and Augie had joined her. Eventually Mrs. Lorentushki did, too.

"A friend taught me this one," Mom had said.

Augie smiled remembering when Mom launched into "Light One Candle" and how Mrs. Lorentushki's gravelly voice came in on the refrain. They had sounded beautiful, all together.

"I could sing 'Light One Candle,' " Augie said.

"That sounds fine."

Mr. Franklin leaned back onto the desk and crossed his arms over his chest. Augie ignored the intent look. He concentrated and imagined candles on the desk instead of a lamp; he imagined Mrs. Lorentushki nervous and in need of cheer, sitting where Mr. Franklin stood; he imagined his mother's eyes shining as they did whenever she sang, and he began.

"Light one candle for the Maccabee children / With thanks that their light didn't die. . . ."

Augie shut his eyes. Inside his head he could hear his mother's voice, high above his, providing the harmony as he sang the melody.

"Light one candle for the pain they endured / When their right to exist was denied. . . ."

He remembered Mrs. Lorentushki coming in with a gentle hum.

"Light one candle for the terrible sacrifice / Justice and freedom demand, / But light one candle for the wisdom to know / When the peacemaker's time is at hand."

He could smell the burning wax. Feel his mother's arm around his shoulder. See the flickering shadows in the corner of the room. He sang the chorus, and his heart swelled. He sang the verses, and they came out right. He didn't hear the words. He felt them.

"Don't let the light go out! / Don't let the light go out! / Don't let the light go out!"

An empty silence filled the room. He opened his eyes and was surprised to see the dirty tiles on the floor, the dusty blackboard on the wall, the worn desks to the side, and Mr. Franklin watching him with an unreadable expression on his face.

"Very good, Augustus. Thank you. Let's head home."

The pit of Augie's stomach felt cold. He had auditioned. What would happen now?

Cornered

THE NEXT MORNING, MR. FRANKLIN posted the list. Mr. Franklin had divided it into groups labeled "Sopranos," "Altos," "Tenors," and "Bass." Kids crowded around to see where they had been placed. Augie hung back.

"Well, well, well, Perfessor," Sergio called. He had given up on "Rich Boy" after Augie had stopped bringing lunch money to school. "Looks like we's gonna be singing next to each other."

The bell rang. Kids scattered. Augie approached the list. Sure enough, under "Tenors" he saw "Sergio Barnaby" immediately followed by "Augustus Boretski." This couldn't be happening. He didn't want to join the chorus. He imagined the torture Sergio was going to put him through—especially if they sang next to each other.

Augie slid into his seat just as the late bell rang. Mr. Franklin seemed to have too much energy that day, giving the class extra notes, roaring enthusiastically about some math problem. Augie wanted to sink under the desk.

At the end of the day, Mr. Franklin handed out a form to Sergio, Augie, Evelyn Carbón, and Fred Washington.

"Have your parents fill these out and return them to me by Friday. You cannot sing until I have their signatures. The first practice will be Monday morning in the cafeteria at seven-thirty sharp."

Augie stuffed the form into his bag. Mom definitely wasn't going to see this.

For the rest of the week, Augie did his best to avoid Mr. Franklin's notice. He kept his head low in class. He stayed away from the music room. He was never first or last in line for anything. The only good part was that Sergio was so engaged in showing off his star material that Fox Tooth and Dwaine had stopped paying attention to Augie. On Friday, Augie actually waited until lunch period to eat. Big mistake.

Augie had just sat down at a table in the cafeteria when Sergio sidled up next to him.

"Well, Perfessor," Sergio said.

Dwaine and Fox Tooth grinned as they placed their

trays across the table. Augie stopped breathing for a second. He was cornered.

"Now that we'll be singin' together, you and I can be buddies," Sergio continued.

Sergio leaned closer, then peered into Augie's bag.

"Buddies share," he said.

Within seconds, Sergio, Dwaine, and Fox Tooth divided Augie's lunch and left him with an empty bag and a growling stomach.

That afternoon was tough. Augie had trouble concentrating—he had skipped breakfast and so now he was really hungry. He felt fuzzy-brained. Mr. Franklin barked at him to pay attention at least twice. After the last bell, all Augie wanted to do was head home, grab some food, and sleep. But Sergio and Dwaine were loitering by the front door. Augie hung back for a minute, hoping they'd leave, but Dwaine saw him. Augie bolted. He was down in the old music room so fast, he was sure Dwaine was still turning around upstairs.

He crumpled onto the desk chair. Whatever energy he'd had was gone. He needed a rest. He put his head down on the desk and shut his eyes. A short rest.

He woke to a gentle hand shaking his shoulder.

"Augustus. It's time to go."

Augie sat bolt upright. Mr. Franklin! Augie scrambled to stand up.

"Sorry. Must have fallen asleep. I'll leave now."

103

"Slow down," Mr. Franklin said. "You're going to forget your jacket."

It had slipped off the desk onto the floor. Augie reached down to pick it up.

"Thanks," he mumbled.

He had almost made it to the door when Mr. Franklin stopped him again.

"You never returned the chorus form."

Augie froze. He didn't know what to say. Mr. Franklin lowered his head a bit and stared at him. Augie squirmed.

"Did you lose it? I can give you another."

"No, sir," Augie said.

Mr. Franklin stared a minute longer.

"I can give you till Monday morning if you forgot."

Augie swallowed. If he said okay, Mr. Franklin was going to expect him Monday morning, and he'd have to explain to him later in the day why he wasn't at practice.

"No, thank you, sir."

Mr. Franklin raised an eyebrow. "You have a solid voice. It will complement the group."

Augie stared at his shoelaces. He heard Mr. Franklin sigh.

"You can't always run away from your problems, Augustus. They have a way of following you."

"Yessir," Augie said, and ran home.

At Louisa's

MOM SEEMED LIVELIER THAN usual. She hovered over Augie's breakfast, whistled while she cleaned up, and seemed to take extra care putting on all her makeup.

"Wear a fresh shirt," she told him.

After lunch, she asked him to comb his hair. Augie immediately became suspicious.

"What's going on?"

"We're going to Philadelphia."

He frowned.

"Don't forget your book," she added.

They were going to the bookstore.

"But, Mom, I haven't finished it."

She shook her head.

"Doesn't matter. I promised Louisa we'd keep her posted. You're the one reading. You do the report."

Mom kept the radio on the whole ride in. Augie stared out the window, wishing he were back on the couch watching cartoons. He dreaded this meeting with the bookstore's owner.

As if to spite him, the ride in was smooth—no traffic delayed them, and Mom found a free parking spot just a block from the store.

"Now be polite," Mom said. "She's done you a favor."

That was true. He hadn't faced the police. But now, much worse than that, he was going to have to give a book report on a book he hadn't finished yet.

Louisa was pleased to see them.

"Ramona and Augie," she said, "have some tea."

Mom smiled. Augie couldn't believe it. Mom drank coffee. Instant. Every day. Why was she smiling about having some stupid tea?

Louisa removed a quilted cover from a blue-and-white china pot, then poured a light brown liquid into matching blue-and-white mugs. Without asking, she added sugar and milk to Augie's.

"A piece of cake?" she offered.

The square she placed on Augie's napkin looked like a slice of dark brown bread, but Augie had promised to be polite, so he took a bite. He was surprised at how moist and sweet the cake tasted. He sipped the tea and felt his insides heat up.

Although he knew Louisa was going to ask him about the book, her peaceful smile put Augie at ease. He wondered if he could ask for a second slice of cake without appearing greedy. Mom dabbed at the corners of her mouth with her napkin. Louisa glanced at Augie and cut him another portion.

"Thank you," Augie said.

Louisa nodded as if to say, *Don't mention it.*

Not until Augie had picked at the last crumbs did Louisa put her cup down.

"I see you have more to read," she said.

This jolted Augie out of his relaxed state. How could she tell? He began to apologize.

"I planned to finish it. . . ."

She raised a hand. Her warm smile never wavered.

"Of course you haven't finished it," she said. "Stories need to be savored."

He wasn't sure what she meant but he nodded anyway.

"You can use one of the couches, if you want," she said. "Your mother and I will talk."

Augie picked up the book. He hadn't expected this, which flustered him even more than when he thought he had to speak about something he hadn't read. He headed for the back of the store and chose an old couch with dark-red-and-blue stripes. The cushions were frayed but very comfortable.

He opened the book. The first page did not disappoint him. Standing in a room with its walls covered by tapestries, a gray-haired gentleman in old-fashioned clothes stared down at a bundle being held by a tall lady. A tiny hand reached out of the bundle toward the couple, and their smiles made even Augie smile in response—they were so happy.

He was about to turn the page when a large man sat down beside him. He looked up with a start. Walter Jones! A moment of happiness at seeing Walter was immediately squashed by his realization that this must have been a setup.

"I see you still have the book," Walter said.

Augie glanced down and shut it. "What are you doing here?"

Walter kept his face blank. "Louisa invited me. You don't seem happy to see me."

"I told you," Augie said. "I don't want a Big Brother."

Augie ignored the pang in his stomach when he said that.

Walter nodded. "Okay. But can you tell me why?"

Walter was neither relaxed nor tense. If Augie had to explain what he saw in one word, he would say Walter was expectant. Walter leaned forward, elbows on his knees, his wide hands dangling in front of him.

Augie scowled. He didn't want to tell Walter anything. Mom was behind this, he was sure. She was the
one who wanted Augie to talk to him. Well, too bad.
Augie planned on saying as little as possible.

"I thought we got along," Walter said.

Augie's frown deepened. They *had* gotten along.
Augie liked Walter. But it didn't matter. Walter was gay.
Sergio, Dwaine, and Fox Tooth would kill Augie when
they found out.

"Did I do anything wrong?" Walter asked.

Why did he have to be so nice?

Augie stood. He needed air. The bookshelves felt as
if they were closing in on him.

Walter crinkled his chin and looked around the
shop.

"How about we step outside?" he said. "Get a little air."

The man seemed to be reading his mind!

"No."

Damn it. Why had Mom brought him here? He
clutched the book and glanced at Walter, who now had
a worried furrow in his brow.

"You okay?" Walter asked.

"Just leave me alone."

Augie said it low and mean. Walter sat back, as if he
had been punched. Augie didn't want to see him like
that. He turned and rushed to the front of the store. He
burst upon Mom and Louisa, who were laughing.

"Let's go," Augie said.

Mom stared at him with surprise.

"But . . ."

Augie wanted out. The shop felt as if it were shrinking. He had to leave before Walter caught up with him.

"We've got to go."

Mom glanced at Louisa, who nodded.

"Give it time," she said.

Mom's eyes looked disappointed—sad, even. Augie didn't want to think about it.

"All right," she said.

She glanced in Walter's direction, but to Augie's relief, the man didn't come out from the stacks. She gathered her purse. Augie led them out the door and toward the car. He waited impatiently while Mom searched for the car keys, as if every second they stayed in Philadelphia was another second when Walter might convince him to change his mind. But Augie's mind was made up.

Mom remained quiet on the way home. She wore a slight frown, but Augie didn't care—he was too angry with her. She had no right to ambush him.

They passed the square at the end of their street. Augie saw the steady flow of traffic: one after another, cars rolled slowly to a stop. A kid approached the car window, and within five seconds, the car continued on its way, only to be replaced by another car. None of the cars were from the neighborhood. These were people from the suburbs getting their drug fix. The contrast with Louisa's bookstore made Augie's stomach lurch.

At home, no one spoke. No one turned on the radio or the TV. Mom began preparing spaghetti for dinner. Augie thought about returning the book to the box behind the couch, but it felt sticky, as if it didn't want to leave his hands. He sat on the recliner, the book on his lap, and he could have sworn that the pages flared.

"Okay!" he said, aggravated by this book with a mind of its own.

"Okay what?" Mom said.

"Nothing," Augie muttered.

Mom would think he was crazy if he told her he thought that the book was magic.

He heard her put a pot down. She came into the living room, drying her hands on a small towel. Augie quickly lifted the book to open it, but she put her hand on the cover, forcing it back down and making him look up.

"You know," she said, "you could have talked to him."

"What do you know?" Augie said.

She wasn't the one who had to deal with the kids in the neighborhood. She wasn't the one who got beat up for no reason, who ran home scared, whose lunch was stolen half the time.

He yanked the book from under her hand. She stared down at him for a moment longer.

"Suit yourself," she said.

She didn't sound angry, which made Augie even angrier. He opened the book roughly to the picture at the front. The gray-haired gentleman and tall lady were still there, but now, instead of staring at the baby, they were looking up out of the page, at Augie, in surprise.

WHEN FAIRIES
FALL IN LOVE

LONG AGO AND FAR AWAY, the fairy Louisa became godmother to the daughter of another powerful king and queen. As the princess grew, the king and queen gave their daughter everything she asked for and allowed her to do whatever she pleased. By the age of nine, she was beautiful and spirited but headstrong.

One gray winter's day, snow fell. She spent the afternoon in the garden, playing, even as the snow changed to sleet and freezing rain. That night, everyone in the castle huddled around fires to keep warm.

"It is good you came in when you did," the princess's nurse told her. "The ground has become slick and dangerous."

"The snow was perfect for a snowman," the princess said. "I shall return to it after my supper."

"You'll catch your death of a cold," the nurse said, and bustled her off to bed.

This angered the princess, who had her mind set on returning outside. She resolved to sneak out of her bed to explore the garden at night, something she had never done before. She had not gone far before she slipped, fell, and twisted her ankle. Several hours passed before her nurse realized she was missing. When they found her, she was frozen.

All feared for the princess's life. The fairy Louisa summoned her craftiest warming spells and nursed the princess day and night until she showed signs of recovery. Although she was exhausted by her efforts, Louisa insisted on announcing the good news personally to the princess's parents.

They were not grateful.

"Your duty as a godmother was to protect her," the king said. "You allowed her to leave her bedchamber in the middle of the night."

The court fell silent after this unjust accusation. Courtiers exchanged uncomfortable glances until a bold gentleman spoke up.

"Your Highnesses. Fairies are powerful but not all-seeing. The fairy Louisa has saved the princess's life, sapping her own strength in the process."

The king and queen refused to listen. They banished Louisa from the court.

Louisa felt bereft. In her many generations as a fairy

godmother, she had never been dismissed, let alone disgraced. And the king and queen's injustice rankled. She sat in the small room that had been hers for so long, contemplating what to do next. A lackey knocked at her door.

"My master begs your pardon but sends this note. I am to wait in the corridor for your response."

He handed Louisa a parchment, which she opened immediately.

To the Most Esteemed Fairy Louisa,
I will be returning to my small landholdings, a few days' journey from here. I do not wish to impose upon your august presence, but while you decide how best to use your wondrous talents, you would be most welcome at my home.

Cordially and humbly,
Michel de Bourgaille

The writer was the very same court gentleman who had come to Louisa's defense. Her curiosity about this brave soul overcame any misgivings she had about the hasty invitation. At the bottom of the note she wrote, "I would be honored. Louisa," and returned it to the servant.

Thus began her friendship with Michel de Bourgaille.

Michel was a middle-aged widower with a grown

son. He had broad interests and commanded the respect of princes and peasants alike, for he was kind and wise. The king had appointed him Lord Mayor of nearby Saint-Jean-de-Limogette. Although he was a good mayor, he did not enjoy the position. He found himself seeking Louisa's counsel often and admiring her wisdom.

Their friendship blossomed into love.

"Marry me," he asked.

"Yes," she replied, but her happiness was laced with sorrow.

Louisa knew that matches between fairies and humans led to heartbreak. The life span of a man is so much shorter than that of a fairy, and a fairy who falls in love with a human does so for all eternity.

The product of their union was a daughter, Louisette, who was half fairy and half human.

Louisette grew into a fine young woman. Her mother taught her what she could of the magic arts—although being half human, Louisette was not magical herself.

"Magic exists everywhere," Louisa said, "you need only look."

Louisette's father taught her writing, Latin, geography, mathematics, and music, all of which she took to with great ease. Her father was proud of her intelligence.

When Michel de Bourgaille died at an advanced age, his holdings passed to his son. The fairy Louisa fell into deep mourning. Everything around her reminded her of Michel and of the pain she would endure for centuries to come. Her only solace, she knew, was to withdraw from human circles and return to the place from which she came. She summoned her daughter.

"I must go among the fairies. But I wish to give you a final gift."

She handed Louisette a small wooden box.

"It shall give you what is needed most," she told her.

Louisette accepted the gift, but she wanted to burn it. What she needed most were her mother and her father, not some magical relic. She buried the box among her things.

Louisette's sadness was so profound that she could no longer bear to be in the home she had known all of her life. She decided to leave the de Bourgaille household. With grace and generosity, her half brother asked her to stay.

"You are truly our father's son," Louisette said. "You are a kind and good man. But it is time for me to find my own way in the world."

Although he had the power to restrain her, her half brother let her go. He loved his half sister but was also afraid of her fairy blood. He supplied her well for the voyage and wished her Godspeed.

Louisette traveled far and wide. She saw deep rivers and snow-peaked mountains. She walked along sun-drenched beaches and traveled across rolling hills richly cultivated by hardworking peasants. She encountered cruel winter storms, met fishermen and hunters, and marveled at ruins left by ancients. After several years, she grew weary of her wanderings and headed back to Saint-Jean-de-Limogette. There, with her half brother's blessing, she opened a small bookshop.

She never opened the box.

The Junior Chorus

MOM WAS THRILLED WHEN Augie showed her the chorus form on Sunday.

"I'm so glad you auditioned," she said.

Augie cringed inside. He hadn't auditioned. At least, he hadn't meant to. But Sergio would target him whether or not he showed up for practice. Since Mr. Franklin had put Augie on the list, he might as well sing. At least that part he liked.

Monday morning dawned cold, the first real cold snap of the season. Augie shivered in his light jacket. The school had turned the heat off for the weekend, so the cafeteria, where they were meeting for practice, wasn't all that much warmer than outside. The fifty or so kids clustered on the stage were stamping their feet, huddling with their arms wrapped around themselves. Most had kept their jackets on.

Sergio showed up with a big, puffy coat and a bright red hat pulled low over his eyebrows.

"Child abuse," he said. "Nothin' but child—"

Augie lost the last word in the loud clanging from the radiators. It sounded like a half dozen bells, all out of tune. One of the fluorescent bulbs flickered and buzzed. Mr. Franklin walked in and frowned.

"Chorus members do not sing in coats," he said.

Kids looked at each other, uncertain.

"But, Mr. Franklin," one girl in fifth grade piped up, "it's cold."

"By the time I'm done with you," Mr. Franklin said, "you'll wish you were in T-shirts."

Kids peeled off their jackets and piled them at the back of the stage. Meanwhile, Mr. Franklin was barking orders.

"Ms. Root, with the sopranos, stage right. Mr. Washington, bass, stage left. Tenors, next to the piano. Ms. Zola, leave your purse with your coat. We are singing, not shopping."

Kids scrambled to their assigned places. Augie managed to keep a fourth grader between himself and Sergio. From his pocket, Mr. Franklin took an odd-looking harmonica with tubes sticking out at different lengths.

"We will first practice singing our scales."

He put the instrument to his lips, furrowed his brow, and brought the instrument back down.

"Mr. Barnaby."

Sergio clicked to attention and saluted. Titters ran through the group. Mr. Franklin ignored them.

"Remove your hat."

"No can do, Mr. Franklin, sir!" Sergio spoke to the back wall, the perfect imitation of an army recruit responding to a drill sergeant. "Bad hair day," he stage-whispered to the kid next to him.

More titters. Augie expected Mr. Franklin to lose it. But Mr. Franklin seemed amused.

"The hat is glued to your ears, Mr. Barnaby?"

Sergio didn't expect that. "Uh, no, sir."

"Attached with a pin, perhaps?"

"No, sir."

"Velcro? Stitches? Duct tape?"

Now the kids were laughing at Sergio. He shook his head uncomfortably.

"Then remove it."

Sergio's face was grim. He pulled the hat straight up, making his short dreadlocks spike up like a porcupine's quills.

Mr. Franklin blew into one of the tubes from his instrument. A clear note carried through the cafeteria, clear despite the buzzing bulb and clanging radiators.

"That is F," Mr. Franklin stated.

He made them all sing that one note.

"Slightly higher, Mr. March. All together."

He blew F again. They sang the note.

"Now G."

Mr. Franklin blew again. The chorus sang the note. He repeated the same drill with each note, up and down the scale, correcting this kid and that one if he was too sharp, or she too flat. Then he blew C and made them do the scale without his prompting.

"Mr. March, you are flat again," he told the sixth grader. He made the boy sing the scale by himself. "Better," Mr. Franklin pronounced.

Then he had them take turns singing each verse of "Do-Re-Mi," dividing the song into voice parts. Augie liked the way "Do" started with the tenors, "Re" dropped with the bass, and "Mi" climbed with the sopranos. He had tuned out all the other noises, and the chorus sounded nice. Very nice. He was surprised when the bell rang.

Mr. Smith, the custodian, a tall, wiry African American man who Augie had long ago decided had the longest fingers in the world, opened the cafeteria doors. Some students poked their heads in.

"Can I let 'em in?" he asked.

Mr. Franklin nodded and turned to the chorus.

"Good work," he said. "We'll meet here again next Monday morning."

Augie was at the back of the stage, fishing for his

jacket among all the others, when he saw Dwaine and Fox Tooth approach Sergio.

"What's with the 'do?" Dwaine asked.

By now, most of Sergio's locks had returned to their usual mop, but a few still stuck out like little antennae.

"Stars are supposed to stand out," Sergio said.

Augie had to admire Sergio's nerve. Both Dwaine and Fox Tooth nodded. Augie fled to the classroom before they noticed him.

If the chorus members expected special treatment in class from Mr. Franklin, they were disappointed. If anything, he seemed harder on them. By lunch he had almost brought Evelyn Carbón to tears, making her redo a math problem three times. Yet Augie felt relieved. He hadn't found trouble and he had had fun.

He loved to sing.

The pattern was set for the following weeks. Before Mr. Franklin arrived, the chorus members shed their coats and hats and grouped themselves as Mr. Franklin had instructed on the first day. Mr. Franklin led them through scales, then taught them songs, dividing them up by voice parts, making them hear themselves sing while listening to each other, too. By the end of the hour, the music had wrapped itself around Augie so that he no longer saw who was singing but only heard their voices.

The hour in chorus was an hour of peace. No matter

where anyone stood, their voices met each other, melded, rose, and fell. The weak ones were carried by the stronger ones. The ones that struggled to stay in key were prodded by the tuneful ones. The ones that roared were hushed by quiet strength. There were no enemies, just voices, working to make themselves mesh.

As early as the second week, Augie could tell whose voice was whose without looking. To his surprise, he learned to listen for Sergio. Despite all his attitude, Sergio could sing. He sang each song right, the first time, every time, with strength and with melody. Augie thought Sergio listened for him, too. Sergio's voice became Augie's companion as they soared and dipped.

Still, Augie avoided Sergio during the rest of the week. Dwaine and Fox Tooth continued to pop up at unexpected moments, and Augie never let his guard down. He was vigilant, even at home. Dwaine kept turning up on the stoop across the street, even though Walter no longer visited. Augie's Big Brother had phoned twice, but, fortunately, Mom had answered both times. Augie had refused to come to the phone. He felt cooped up, too afraid to leave the house on weekends, except with his mom. But once a week he had some real music in his life, and that kept him from going crazy.

At the end of the fourth week, Mr. Franklin announced that they were to perform a holiday concert.

"Starting immediately after Thanksgiving, we will practice twice a week."

Annie raised her hand.

"Yes, Ms. Zola?"

"Will there be any solos?"

Mr. Franklin pursed his lips. "We shall see."

Dwaine and Fox Tooth had walked in at that moment. They thumped Sergio on the back when he came down from the stage.

"You're going to get your own song!" Fox Tooth said.

"Sure thing!" Sergio replied.

But Augie knew Sergio's voice well enough by now to catch the slight tremor in his bravado.

Thanksgiving

THE WEDNESDAY BEFORE THANKSGIVING, Mr. Franklin was late for class. The principal, Ms. Cofrancesco, showed up in his place. She wore a crisp blue-and-gray suit, with a white shirt that highlighted the dark brown of her skin. Augie sometimes wondered how she kept her hair in that perfect bell shape.

Kids murmured to one another.

"Settle down," Ms. Cofrancesco told them. "Mr. Franklin has asked that you read pages forty-six to fifty-two of your social studies text and be ready to discuss it when he arrives."

"Discuss," the kids understood, meant that Mr.

Franklin planned to ask a host of questions that students had better know the answers to. Even Fox Tooth read in earnest. About ten minutes later, Mr. Franklin breezed through the door looking very happy.

"Thank you, Ms. Cofrancesco."

The principal gave Mr. Franklin what Augie thought was a knowing smile.

"Please put your books away," Mr. Franklin told the class. "We will be having a special assembly, in the cafeteria. Line up quietly."

They lined up, but not quietly. Everyone was curious. What was going on? Mr. Franklin led the way; Ms. Cofrancesco took up the rear. Even from the middle of the line, Augie heard Mr. Franklin humming.

When they reached the cafeteria, the piano was in two pieces. Its back was leaning against the stage wall, while the guts—long strings stretched from peg to peg—faced the cafeteria. Chairs lined the front of the stage, most of them taken up by other sixth graders at Willard.

"Today we will learn about frequency and sound," Mr. Franklin announced.

From the other side of the piano, a smaller, wiry version of Mr. Franklin, dressed in brown pants and a plaid shirt, stepped forward.

"I would like to introduce you to Samuel Franklin," Mr. Franklin continued, "my brother."

"You may call me Sam," Mr. Franklin's brother said. He bowed. "I am a musician."

For the next twenty minutes, Sam discussed vibrations and sound, the different lengths of wires and types of sounding boards, and a whole lot about music that mostly went over everyone's heads. Augie's class paid attention, though. This was a lot better than being quizzed about their social studies text.

"Do you have any questions?" Sam asked.

Fred Washington's hand floated up. "What's in that suitcase next to the piano?"

Sam grinned. "My tools."

He opened it up. Inside was a gleaming set of wrenches, some wire, hammers, felts, and tuning forks.

"You're a piano tuner!" Evelyn Carbón cried out, sounding disgusted. "You said you were a musician."

Sam might have looked hurt if his mouth wasn't having such a hard time keeping down his grin.

"I am both," he said. "One of my jobs has to pay the bills."

Then, fast and cheerful, he deployed his tools, made adjustments to the strings, listened to his fork, and nodded.

"I was finishing up when Arthur suggested I show you how it works."

For a moment, the students struggled to connect "Arthur" to Mr. Franklin.

"Why don't you show our sixth graders what you can play?" Mr. Franklin said.

Ms. Cofrancesco looked alarmed. "We only have funds for the tuning," she said.

"No charge, ma'am," Sam said. "I have to play it to see if it's tuned right."

He started with a classical piece that sounded a lot like "Twinkle, Twinkle, Little Star." Dwaine made a show of falling asleep. Fox Tooth did the same. Sam pretended not to notice.

"This is variations on 'Ah, vous dirais-je, Maman,' by Wolfgang Amadeus Mozart," Sam said, "a great composer."

"A dead white guy," Sergio snorted.

Sam grinned, never pausing in his performance. "A dead, *brilliant* white guy," he said.

Then the music changed. First the tempo sped up. Chords became fuller and wove around the tune. Next, the song became quiet and cheerful, then bombastic and loud. It kept changing as he played. It turned into a folk song, a sad song, it lost itself in a beautiful sweep of chords, and then it reappeared rich and then poor. It became soft and soothing, then ran so fast it couldn't keep up with itself. Sam moved up and down the piano keys, until finally, the chords separated, the left and right hands were independent, and the song turned inside out into a breathtaking rendition of the blues.

Every kid in the room sat in rapt attention as he ended with a tiny tinkle. There were two whole beats of silence before the sixth graders roared into applause.

Sam stood and bowed.

"No Mozart person wrote that thing," Sergio said.

"Actually, he did," Sam said, "except for the last part." He lifted his hand to his face and leaned forward. "That was me."

"It's all the same song," Jamil March said, "isn't it?"

"It is," Sam said. "Mr. Mozart called it 'variations.' In jazz we call it improvisations, until we write them down."

Sergio seemed surprised by what he had heard—he didn't have his I'm-too-smart-for-this-crap look on. Dwaine and Fox Tooth appeared clueless.

"Thank you, Sam," Mr. Franklin said. "We'll return to our classrooms now."

"Sure thing," Sam said. "Don't work 'em too hard."

Whether because of Sam's admonition, or the fact that the half day of school was nearly over, or that Mr. Franklin had thoughts of his own Thanksgiving, the next few hours were the easiest the class had experienced all year.

"Enjoy your holidays!" Mr. Franklin said.

He hadn't assigned any homework!

The goodwill seemed to carry to Dwaine, Sergio, and Fox Tooth. They allowed Augie to leave as they lingered, talking about some plans. Augie couldn't wait to be home!

Thanksgiving was special. Mom stayed in her pajamas all morning, and the two of them lounged on Augie's unmade bed watching the Macy's Thanksgiving Day Parade on television. She made vats of popcorn drizzled with real butter. Dinner came from the diner—turkey, cranberry sauce, stuffing, candied yams—but Mom made the mashed potatoes. "I like to put in fried onions," she had told him once. And for the occasion, Mom always bought a whole pumpkin pie.

Mom didn't like pumpkin pie. She ate the vanilla ice cream and left her token slice on the plate. The pie was strictly for Augie. Over the weekend he'd finish it off, savoring every mouthful. It was Mom's unspoken annual gift for him, and he relished it.

On Friday, they drove into Germantown, a Philadelphia neighborhood, to visit Phillip and Isabella for an hour. They were Mom's parents, Augie's grandparents. When Augie was seven or eight, he had begun to notice that other families got together for the holiday meal.

"Why don't we have Thanksgiving with Phillip and Isabella?" he asked.

"Other families have their ways," Mom said, "and we have ours."

Over the years, Augie pestered her about it until she finally told him, "Phillip and Isabella don't approve of me."

The story came in dribs and drabs.

Phillip and Isabella were set in their ways. They had immigrated from old Czechoslovakia and lived their lives here much the same way people had lived their lives there. Isabella cooked and kept house. Phillip worked all day at his butcher shop. Isabella woke every morning before anyone else and cooked a full breakfast so that Phillip could be at work by seven o'clock. He was home in time for dinner, and he expected it to be ready when he walked in the door. "I bring the meat into the house. It should be cooked when I get there," he'd say. Isabella was never late. She took whatever package of white butcher paper he brought home—meat for the next day's supper—and stashed it in the fridge. While Phillip washed up from that day's work, she started serving: noodles, potatoes, sauerkraut, vegetables, and of course meat, cooked perfectly. When the meal was done, Phillip left the dishes on the table and sat in front of the TV until bedtime.

As a teenager, Mom had wanted to escape. Howie Boretski promised a way out. He had a twinkle in his eye. He smoked cigarettes. He spent summers as a roadie for a carnival, lying about his age to get hired. He swept Augie's mom off her feet. She was sixteen and became pregnant. When Isabella and Phillip found out, they threw her out. That's when Mom and Howie moved to Camden.

"Then why do we visit them every Friday after Thanksgiving?" Augie asked.

"That was Mama's doing," Mom said. "Pops wouldn't let me take part in any family activity, but Mama convinced him that even acquaintances are allowed to visit sometimes. She chose the day after Thanksgiving."

Augie didn't enjoy this year's visit any more than the ones in the past. Phillip and Isabella's house was too warm, the heat blasting Augie away. Phillip wore a stained T-shirt and watched football. Isabella served juice and cookies but treated her guests formally. She made them sit in uncomfortable chairs in the dining room.

"How do you do?" "Where are you employed now, Ramona?" "What grade are you in, Augustus?" "It feels like an early winter this year."

Phillip only grunted "hello" when Mom spoke to him directly, and he acted as if Augie didn't exist. He interrupted all the time as if no conversation were taking place, demanding something or other from Isabella.

"Another beer." "Bring the cookies."

Isabella stopped in mid-sentence, brought him whatever he wanted, and returned to the stilted chitchat until Mom announced they had to go. The only part of the visit that wasn't uncomfortable was Isabella's hug for Mom. That was real.

Augie said that to Mom on the ride home.

"She says a lot that way," Mom said.

"She didn't *say* anything," Augie said.

"She didn't have to," Mom replied.

Augie wondered what Isabella had said. Mom was humming in a low voice as she directed the old Buick through traffic. The hug must have said something nice, because Mom seemed happy.

Augie settled back into his seat. Thanksgiving was the best holiday of all.

Trapped Inside

MOM WORKED THE DAY shift on Saturday. She left some food for Augie in the fridge and strict instructions not to leave the house.

"There was a shooting yesterday, three blocks away," she said. "I don't want you near there."

If one gang member was shot, then his crew would want revenge. Although no one was going to mistake Augie for a gang member, if he happened to walk near someone who was, he might get hit by mistake. He knew he wasn't safe outside today.

Augie watched television until the morning cartoons petered out. He felt lonely and wished there were somewhere to go. He remembered how he hadn't liked bowling when Walter had taken him. But even that beat sticking around this tiny apartment all day.

He turned on the radio in hopes of finding something worth singing along to when he heard a crash out front. He rushed to the window.

A large silver car with a red roof had rear-ended a smaller, brown one. A slim man leaped out of the front car and started screaming obscenities. A very large woman slowly climbed out of the rear car, holding a cell phone to her ear. Neighbors peeked their heads out of doorways and looked through barred windows. For the next hour, they watched the two argue while waiting for the police. Nothing terrible happened. No one pulled a gun. No one raised a fist. They just yelled and waited. Augie never left the window, fascinated and relieved at the same time. He was disappointed when the cars finally pulled away, leaving behind shards of red plastic from a broken brake light. He wondered how long it would take before they were swept to the side of the road and ground down to join the rest of the shards that littered the street.

The phone rang. The noise made him jump. It must be Mom. He picked up the receiver.

"Hello?"

"Hey."

Walter!

"How are you doing?" Walter asked.

Silence.

Walter, Augie thought. His emotions tumbled. Why was Walter calling?

"You still there?" Walter said.

"Y-yeah," Augie said.

"I just wanted to wish you a happy Thanksgiving."

"Thanks."

Safe. Augie knew how to give short, safe replies. He focused. Answer what Walter asked, he told himself, no more. He could get through this.

"You doing okay?" Walter asked.

Augie swallowed.

"Yeah," he said. "I'm okay."

"You're still reading that book?"

"Yeah."

"Keep at it," Walter said.

What business was it of his? Augie thought.

"I hope you don't mind that I called," Walter continued.

Augie paused. Did he mind?

"No. It's okay."

"Well, take care. All right?"

"Yeah. Sure."

He hung up and took a breath. He realized he hadn't wished Walter a happy Thanksgiving in return.

Augie looked around the small apartment. He was trapped in here, by himself, in a city too dangerous to go and explore. While Walter was . . . What was Walter doing right now?

He kicked the side of the couch.

He remembered Louisa's book. Of course. Why hadn't he taken it out before? He pulled it out, eager to see the picture on the front page.

The scene made his heart race. On a dark street, a woman in a long cloak pulled over her head led an old horse away from a stone house. She clutched her cowl and glanced backward, fear lining her face. Her shoulders curved forward as if she were under a great burden. A man stood in the doorway, counting coins from a small bag with glee in his eyes.

After a second's hesitation, Augie let the book open to where he had left off.

LOUISETTE

DE BOURGAILLE

THE HALF-FAIRY LOUISETTE DID well for herself in her small bookshop at Saint-Jean-de-Limogette. She was much respected, as her parents had been before her. The learned and not-so-learned came into her shop and discussed this matter or the other for hours. Louisette felt at peace. She had found her calling. Years passed in this way.

But times in the Old World were hard. Peasants were poor and ill-used. Burghers grumbled that their power did not match their wealth. And people feared anyone different from themselves. Although eighty, Louisette was still a twenty-five-year-old in body, thanks to her fairy blood. In the seventeenth century, when people were old and wrinkled at forty, Louisette's eternal youth made people whisper. She became a target for those who see evil, even when there is none.

Then pestilence began traveling the land. Fear walked in every household. Old and young died at a terrifying rate. People needed to blame someone for this horror.

"It's the half-fairy," they murmured. "She's to blame for this unholiness."

Men and women suddenly fell silent as she walked by. One of her windows was broken by a rock. Someone left a dead rat on her doorstep. No one came into her shop.

One night, the baker's wife knocked at her door.

"Mademoiselle," she said, "I heard talk in the market today. Some say they wish to burn your house. Others say they wish to burn *you*."

Louisette shuddered. She had to flee.

"Thank you for the warning," she said. "I know you have given it to me at your own peril."

The baker's wife tightened her shawl around her shoulders.

"Your mother once nursed my grandfather when he was gravely ill. Our family owes you a debt of gratitude."

"Your debt is paid," Louisette replied.

Louisette packed only what she could carry. As she pulled out an old, warm cloak to wear, she discovered the box her mother had given her. Louisette had forgotten it. She dusted it off and recalled her mother's words: "It shall give you what is needed most." Louisette ran her fingers over the warm wood, hesitating for a moment before opening it.

Inside was a tattered leather pouch, empty to the touch.

A knock came at her door. Outside stood a peasant. She had paid him an absurd price to hire his horse so that she could ride to the next town, where a friend had offered her shelter.

"The townsfolk are restless," the peasant said. "I don't want to risk the horse."

"But I have paid you," she replied.

"Not enough," he said.

Louisette felt desperate. She knew she had to leave before the townspeople turned into a mob.

"I will double the fee," she said, "and buy your horse outright."

The peasant chewed, his mouth puckered into a frown.

"Pay me five times the fee, and he is yours."

The sum the man demanded equaled all the gold Louisette possessed—the price of a prize stallion, not a run-down plow horse. But Louisette had no choice, so she handed over the coins. She wrapped herself in the cloak, pocketed the leather pouch, and, after a moment's hesitation, took the box.

I now have an empty leather pouch, she thought. *Is that what I really need?*

Although the peasant's horse was even more beaten down than Louisette had expected, he was docile and delivered her safely to her friend.

"You may stay," her friend told her, "but not for long. Word has escaped that you have come here. Folks fear you and will do you harm."

Louisette knew her friend was right. But a horse required fodder, and she needed food and shelter. How was she going to provide for herself? She looked at the leather pouch, flat and empty.

"What use is an empty purse?" she said.

Her friend asked, "Have you looked inside?"

"No," Louisette admitted.

She pulled the bag open. Lo and behold, a ruby sat at the bottom. Louisette took it out, marveling at its beauty. The stone was small but reflected a brilliant red in the firelight. She closed the fingers of her other hand around the outside of the purse, and again, it felt empty. When she looked back inside, a new ruby sat at the bottom.

And so Louisette traveled. She journeyed from kingdom to kingdom, selling her rubies discreetly in large towns and living humbly. Her only companion was the old horse who carried her faithfully. She remained fearful of crowds and worried that people might discover her true nature. And so she moved on, until eventually she crossed the Channel and came to London. She had finally reached a city large and anonymous enough that she could settle in unnoticed. She opened a shop, and her presence for seventy-five years in the same alley did not raise anyone's curiosity.

Her loneliness, however, coupled with the city's filth and congestion, wore away at her soul.

Louisette heard of settlements in the colonies across the ocean—tales of large expanses of land and of the rough life of settlers. She remembered the farmworkers from her childhood who revered her mother and treated Louisette with kindness.

She readied herself for another voyage.

The ship landed in Philadelphia. The young town bustled with life and a sense of openness that Louisette had never encountered before. She set up a small shop that combined book sales with a subscription lending library, and soon she found eager customers. Among them was a young man. His sharp features and receding hairline made him look a bit like a bird of prey, but he was clever, well read, and eager to learn about new ideas and strange phenomena. Louisette liked him right away.

"Have tea with me," she said.

The young man accepted her invitation.

Although ancient in human terms, Louisette appeared to people as a very handsome, middle-aged woman. The insightful young man grasped that she had wisdom beyond his ken and found himself attracted to her. His visits became more frequent, their talk more intimate. For a while they became lovers. But the colonies offered too little education for a wealthy merchant's son, and the young man's father sent him abroad to complete his studies.

"I will never forget you," he told her.

Louisette smiled at his youthful sincerity.

"Godspeed," she said.

The product of their brief and happy union was a daughter. Louisette never told the young man about the baby. She did not feel the need. In several years, she knew, his father would find him a young, charming, and suitable wife. And although Louisette enjoyed the man's company, her love for him was not deep.

She named her daughter Marie-Louise de Bourgaille. Louisette had found the most magical gift she had ever encountered in her long life—the love a parent holds for her child.

Troubles

LOUISETTE'S STORY STUCK WITH Augie. Why had the town wanted to kill her, just because she was part fairy? Hadn't she helped them? And it wasn't fair that she had to hide who she was, everywhere she went.

On Sunday, Augie mulled over the story as he helped Mrs. Lorentushki put up the Christmas decorations. His thoughts were interrupted by Sergio, Fox Tooth, and Dwaine, who decided to heckle Augie as he strung lights across the porch roof on a ladder.

"There's a tangle," Dwaine called.

"Missed a post, Perfessor," Sergio said.

"Don't stick no fingers in no sockets," Fox Tooth added.

Augie tried to ignore them.

"Go away," Mrs. Lorentushki yelled. "Leave this place or I call the police."

The boys laughed at the old woman, but at least they left. The good feelings Augie had gathered over the long weekend were beginning to evaporate.

On Monday, Mr. Franklin announced the songs they'd be singing for the holiday show—they already knew all but one. Yet nothing the chorus did that morning was right. They were all off key or off tempo. Kids kept mixing up the words. And Mr. Franklin, now directing from the piano, exploded at every mistake, occasionally banging on the keys in frustration. Even Augie, who usually had no problems, took a hit.

"More energy, Mr. Boretski. You're not digesting a turkey, you're entertaining a crowd!"

More than halfway through, Ms. Cofrancesco showed up. She listened for a few minutes as Audrey Motts kept breaking at the last notes of a verse.

"Ms. Motts, concentration!"

"Excuse me, Mr. Franklin," Ms. Cofrancesco said.

Mr. Franklin frowned at the interruption.

"Five-minute break," he announced.

The kids were relieved. Ms. Cofrancesco walked Mr. Franklin to the side and spoke in hushed tones. Augie couldn't make out her words, but Mr. Franklin furrowed his brow and had a look that every kid in class knew meant they had better be very quiet that day. Mr. Franklin murmured something back, although Augie thought it sounded more like a series of growls. Ms. Cofrancesco didn't like the reply. She started sounding angry, too. Their voices rose.

"I'm donating my time," Mr. Franklin said. "All I ask is a little space and you won't give it to me."

"You don't balance the books, Arthur," Ms. Cofrancesco replied. "We can't afford the oil!"

"When will this school understand that you can't teach unless you give children something to learn?"

"We all support what you're doing—"

"Like hell you do!"

Mr. Franklin stomped away. Ms. Cofrancesco looked even angrier than before.

"Attention," Mr. Franklin told the students. "I have been informed by our principal that our music practices are straining the school budget."

Ms. Cofrancesco looked like she was about to protest, but Mr. Franklin barreled ahead.

"It seems that the school has to turn up the heat, and Mr. Smith has to come in an hour earlier because we are here. As a result, Ms. Cofrancesco wants us to stop practicing."

A chorus of protests came from the kids.

"No way!" Evelyn Carbón cried out.

"Not fair!" Jamil March said.

"We bust our butts," Sergio said louder than the rest.

"Yeah," Fred Washington said.

Ms. Cofrancesco clearly hadn't expected this. She tried to back out of the room. Mr. Franklin didn't let her.

"These students have worked very hard," he told her. "I think you owe them an explanation."

Ms. Cofrancesco gave Mr. Franklin a dark look. Her voice sounded shaky.

"As Mr. Franklin said," she began, "the cost for heating the school earlier than eight-thirty a.m. is not in our budget—"

"The heat's crap anyway," Sergio interrupted. "The place stays cold and it makes a racket."

"Be that as it may," she said, trying to regain her composure, "Mr. Smith's early arrival means we have to pay overtime—"

"All he does is let us in," Evelyn Carbón interrupted in turn. "Any fool can do that."

When had she become so bold? Augie wondered.

"Now, now, students," Mr. Franklin said. He was reining in the kids, but Augie could tell he enjoyed Ms. Cofrancesco's discomfort. "Let's be civil."

"You want us to be civil," Sergio said, "but she's not. We're the ones comin' in early, memorizin' stuff, puttin' on a good show, and now she's pullin' the plug."

Ms. Cofrancesco's brown cheeks flushed under her makeup.

"Maybe we could work out some sort of compromise," Ms. Cofrancesco said. "But I cannot okay extra heating costs or more overtime."

"Yeah. No heat. No Mr. Smith. What kind of compromise is that?" Jamil March said.

Mr. Franklin scratched his chin. "Not a bad one, perhaps," he said.

He turned to Ms. Cofrancesco. "Mr. Barnaby is correct. The heating system makes distracting noises, while taking a long time to warm up."

Sergio looked a little worried.

"Since you cannot turn it on, don't. We'll practice in our jackets."

The kids looked at each other, not believing what they were hearing.

"And Ms. Carbón is also correct. I could let the students into the school with my key, thereby obviating the need for Mr. Smith."

"I don't know, Arthur," Ms. Cofrancesco said.

"Mr. Barnaby was also right in that the students are doing a terrific job," Mr. Franklin added.

That was the first time the kids heard Mr. Franklin say so. Augie felt a surge of pride.

"Something good has begun to roll," Mr. Franklin continued. "It isn't time to put on the brakes."

Ms. Cofrancesco stared at him for a minute. The students watched in silence. She turned her head slowly to the students, then back to Mr. Franklin.

"Okay," she said, "but I will hold you responsible for that hour."

"Gladly," Mr. Franklin said.

Ms. Cofrancesco stood there for a second longer. Augie wondered whether she planned to say anything more. But she didn't. She left. Mr. Franklin deflated when she was out of sight.

"As you have gathered," he said, "the school will not turn up the heat for us, nor provide us any support." He looked at the kids with concern in his sad eyes. "It won't be the most pleasant way to conduct practices."

"Wasn't pleasant to start with," Sergio whispered to his neighbor.

If Mr. Franklin heard this, he ignored it.

"I will not hold it against any student if he or she decides to quit."

A few kids murmured to each other, but Mr. Franklin pressed on.

"For those who decide to stay, you will need to wear warm clothing and be very punctual. I will stand by the front door from seven-twenty to seven-twenty-nine, but not a minute longer."

The first bell rang. The students were supposed to head to their classrooms, but no one moved. Mr. Franklin swallowed.

"You are all good singers. In the last few weeks, I have looked forward to this precious hour when I can listen to you perform. I hope we will continue as much as we can."

He folded the sheet music away. Sergio piped up, full power in his voice.

"You ain't seen nothin' yet!"

If Augie didn't know better, he'd have sworn there was moisture in Mr. Franklin's eyes.

Louisa's Box

"I'M GLAD THE KIDS showed up."

"Every one of 'em," Augie said, "and on time, too."

Augie and Mom were driving into Philadelphia to visit the bookstore again, and Augie was recounting what had happened at Thursday's chorus rehearsal.

"We were cold, though."

Even Mr. Franklin had kept his coat on until about eight-fifteen, when the heating had started in earnest. Augie had never taken his off—he had worn his light jacket. His two-year-old coat was too small. Mom had promised him a new one.

"As soon as I get my Christmas bonus," she had said.

He hadn't complained, though. No one had complained, especially after Sergio's warning: "Anyone who says it's cold gets warmed up by me."

If Mr. Franklin had been pleased that not a single kid had dropped out, he did not say anything. He just worked them harder than ever. He had made them practice two old songs and had redivided the parts on a third.

"Mr. Franklin said that we're going to start rehearsing four times a week," Augie said.

"Sure sounds like a lot of practice," Mom said.

"We need it."

They did. Not because they couldn't sing, but because they had so much to learn, so many parts to nail. Mr. Franklin wasn't content with everyone singing together in key, on tempo, the words right. He wanted more: layers of sound, jumping in and out. Augie couldn't imagine they'd get it all straight in time.

"We still have one more song to learn," Augie said.

Mom nodded. She had been driving around, trying to find a parking space. She finally found one, three blocks away. The wind was wicked and bit into Augie, making him shiver. His glasses fogged up when they entered the shop.

"Hello, Augie. Hello, Ramona."

Louisa's smile was warm, but still Augie shivered. He wiped his lenses on his sleeve. He wasn't quite sure why they were here. Mom had said Louisa had called during the week and wanted to see them. She had promised that Walter wasn't going to be there—although, secretly, he was disappointed not to see him.

They sat at the counter.

"I found something the other day," Louisa said, "and I realized it belonged to Augie."

Augie glanced at his mom.

"I didn't leave anything . . . ," he began.

Louisa smiled. "No, no. Let me show you."

Louisa rummaged behind the counter. When she straightened, she held a small wooden box, which she then placed in front of Augie. He was sure his eyes were bulging. The box's wood gleamed under the light. The hinges shone a pale pink. It looked exactly how he imagined the box in the stories might look. How could that be?

"I was going to wait," Louisa said to Augie, "but I spoke with Ramona, and she agreed you could use this sooner."

Mom smiled, too—a genuine Mom smile. Louisa must have convinced her that this would be worth the trip to Philly.

Louisa opened the lid.

If Augie expected shining light to pour out, he was disappointed. There was no twinkling music, no stardust, no exotic smell. Louisa pulled out a package wrapped in red-and-green tissue paper. Augie wondered how it had fit inside the box.

"An early merry Christmas to you," she said, handing him the package.

When Augie unwrapped the present, he realized that the tissue paper was white. The tartan vest inside was what shone grass green, fire-engine red, and perfect blue, with yellow threads running here and there. The colors were deep and rich. And bright. He stared at it. This time from shock.

If Louisa saw his uncertainty, she pretended not to notice.

"It's flannel," she explained.

"Try it on!" Mom said.

Augie didn't have a choice. He took off his jacket and put the vest on. He noticed that the inside was bright red. The vest felt soft, very soft. And very, very warm. It fit perfectly.

Augie took a deep breath. He had the sensation of being wrapped in an old blanket: safe, warm, and loved.

"Thank you!" he said. He meant it.

Louisa smiled and shut the lid. Perhaps it was her easy welcome, or maybe the vest made him bolder. Whatever the reason, he didn't hesitate.

"Can I ask you something?" he said.

"Of course."

Mom gave him a warning glance, but Louisa put a hand on hers and Mom seemed to relax.

"The book I'm reading," he said.

She nodded, encouraging him.

"Is it magic?"

She raised her eyebrows, but neither in surprise nor in annoyance—more as if she was considering the matter. Mom, on the other hand, looked as if she was ready to apologize.

"As magical as anything else," Louisa said.

Augie frowned. He didn't understand the answer.

"But the stories," he said, "are they true?"

At this, Louisa nodded.

"True, but not always accurate."

His frown deepened. Mom jumped in and patted Augie's vest.

"This is so generous of you. Thank you."

Louisa turned to Mom. "Please. I found it and didn't know what to do with it. I'm glad it will have some use."

At that moment the front bells chimed, and a deliveryman arrived laden with a large package.

"If you'll excuse me," Louisa said.

The man placed the package on the counter while Mom nudged Augie out of the way. They went over to a section of the store where Louisa kept children's books. A beanbag chair sat in one corner next to several wooden ones and a low table, all the right size for small children.

"Wow," Mom said. "I wish there was a place like this when I was a kid."

She began flipping through a picture book, a happy smile on her face. Louisa beckoned to Augie from the front counter. Mom stood with the book, mouthing words, oblivious to everything else, so he walked back to Louisa without her. Louisa had opened the package, and she was now emptying it, taking out books with deep-brown-and-red covers.

"So," she said, "where are you in our book?"

Augie swallowed.

"I've read Louisette's story."

"Ah."

Louisa took out a rag and began dusting the volumes. She obviously expected more from him. Augie wasn't sure what to say.

"Something about it kind of bothered me."

"Oh?"

She was making a neat pile on the back shelf. Augie focused on what he thought of Louisette's story.

"It's the way she had to hide," he said. "Just 'cause she was part fairy, she couldn't let anyone know what she was."

"And what was she?"

"A really cool woman. Someone who had traveled and was nice. She never hurt anyone."

"Yet people tried to hurt her," Louisa said.

"Yeah."

"Not very fair."

"No," Augie agreed.

Louisa nodded. She had finished dusting the last book.

"Could you help me with these?" she asked.

She handed Augie a small stack of the books while she picked up the rest. Augie followed her down to a bookcase, where she shelved them next to other red-and-brown volumes. Mom came by at that point, looking for Augie.

"We should head back," she said.

Louisa nodded. "Thank you for your help."

Augie flushed. As Mom turned toward the door, Louisa placed her hand on Augie's arm.

"Remember what you told me."

Augie felt confused again. Louisa seemed to speak in riddles.

He ran to catch up with Mom. The walk back to the car wasn't as bone-chilling as it had been on the way to the store—the vest kept him warm under his jacket.

"Do you think people always hide who they are?" Augie asked as the car pulled into traffic.

Mom glanced at him briefly. "Is that what you were talking about with Louisa?"

Augie frowned and stared out the side window. "We talked about the book."

They drove in silence for a few blocks, heading toward the bridge back to Camden. Then, to Augie's surprise, Mom answered his question.

"I think people hide what they have to."

Augie turned to look at her. She was concentrating on the road, avoiding a bicyclist.

"I don't hide who I am from you," he said.

She gave him a quick, wry smile. "Even when you go out when you're not supposed to?"

That made him angry. "Yeah. Well, I told you about it, remember? And that's how we got to meet Louisa."

"True," Mom said.

She sounded distracted. Maybe because she was merging onto a highway. Or maybe because she thought he did hide things from her.

"Hey, I don't hide things like Walter does."

She gave him a quick, surprised look. "Walter?"

"Yeah, Walter."

She furrowed her eyebrows in worry.

"What has he been hiding?" she said.

"That he's gay!"

Her laugh sounded relieved, but it only irritated Augie.

"He's never hidden that," she said.

Augie crossed his arms and stared straight ahead. Mom shook her head.

"Augie, he doesn't *hide* it. It's not the first thing he tells you. But why should it be? If you ask, he's honest." She slowed behind a truck. "He's always up front about who he is. It's one of the things I like about him."

He looked at Mom, worried.

"You like him?"

She nodded. "What's not to like? He's a nice, smart, generous man."

Augie frowned. Mom was right, of course, and that made him uncomfortable.

"Look, honey, why don't you give Walter another chance?"

Augie thought about that the rest of the drive home. He shivered as they passed the drug dealers at the square, and was glad when he saw the safe yellow house that Mrs. Lorentushki kept so neat, sandwiched between a blue one and a brown one. He saw Dwaine about a block away, throwing a soda can at a stray cat. He reminded him of the villagers who wanted to hurt Louisette because she was different. Stupid Dwaine. He had missed the cat and was now kicking another can down the street and spitting on stoops along the way.

Dwaine was the reason Augie had told Walter to leave. Walter had done nothing wrong—in fact, he had tried to help. He would help Augie again, if he let him. Keeping him out of his life because of narrow-minded, bullying Dwaine was stupid.

In their apartment, Augie hung his jacket on the small peg by the door. He looked down at the vest he still wore, remembering Louisa's kindness. He hesitated for a second. He thought of the villagers chasing

Louisette out of town and remembered Dwaine's look as he threw the soda can at the cat. Why was he letting Dwaine choose his friends?

"Do you still have Walter's phone number?" he asked.

Jesse

TALKING TO WALTER WAS hard. Augie wasn't sure what to say and mostly gave one-word answers to Walter's questions. But Walter didn't seem to mind. He suggested they visit Pear Hill Park on Sunday.

"Just to be sure you still want a Big Brother," he said.

Walter had made it easy. Augie sighed. He wondered whether he should go through with it.

When Walter showed up, no one was on the stoop across the street. Augie ducked into his truck in a hurry and sat low in the seat.

"Good to see you," Walter said.

"Yeah," Augie said.

No mushy stuff, Augie thought.

"Are those guys still after you?" Walter asked.

Augie peeked over the edge of the window. They had driven a few blocks beyond Dwaine's territory. He sat straighter.

"Some," he said.

Actually, they had been okay lately, ever since the chorus had begun practicing in earnest. He figured Sergio might have something to do with that. But he wasn't sure. And he didn't want to talk about it with Walter. Not yet.

"Where are we going?" Augie asked.

This wasn't the same route they had taken the last time they went to the park.

"The Pear Hill Hardware Store," Walter said. "I promised Roger I'd give Jesse a run."

Now Augie was worried. He hadn't expected them to pick up a dog. When he had met Jesse, they had been in Mrs. Lorentushki's apartment. The dog had stayed under the kitchen table while Mrs. Lorentushki took care of Augie's cuts and bruises. Spending time up close with the dog for a couple of hours was another thing altogether.

Walter must have seen his concern.

"Don't worry," he said. "Jesse's a pussycat."

"He wasn't when those guys checked out your truck."

Walter smiled.

"Jesse wouldn't have harmed them. He saw something move outside the window and probably thought it was one of the rabbits he used to chase at the track."

"Track?"

"Oh yeah. Jesse was rescued."

Walter explained how Jesse used to be a racing dog. People trained greyhounds to chase mechanical rabbits around a track. Gamblers placed bets on them. The dogs spent almost all of their lives in cages, and after a few years were killed.

"You mean they kill dogs when they are only a few years old?" Augie said.

Walter nodded.

"That's just awful," Augie said.

"I know. But there are rescue groups now that try to save as many of them as they can. Roger adopted Jesse that way."

Jesse was lucky, Augie thought.

At the Pear Hill Hardware Store they were met by a white man with dark hair, as tall as Walter but less broad. He smiled and extended his hand to Augie.

"I'm Roger Hoover."

This was Walter's partner, another gay man. After a second's hesitation, Augie gave his hand. The handshake was solid and friendly.

"We're here to pick up Jesse," Walter said.

Roger brought them round back. At the side of

the yard was a long, narrow enclosure. At one end it opened up to a doghouse, a large bowl of water, and a bunch of chew toys. The run itself might have had grass at one point, but now was worn down to brown earth. As soon as Jesse heard them coming, he began to bark furiously.

When Roger opened the door, Jesse slobbered on him thoroughly, then jumped on Walter.

"I had to pen him for a few minutes," Roger said. "Some customers are nervous around dogs."

Augie hoped that Jesse wouldn't jump on him, too. To his relief, the dog simply sniffed his hand. *Don't bite me,* he thought.

"Give him a pat," Walter said. "He'll appreciate it."

Augie hesitated. He placed his hand on the dog's neck and gave him one stroke. Jesse wagged his tail and cocked his head. He was so tall that his head reached Augie's chest.

"He's really gentle," Walter assured him.

Augie nodded but kept an eye on the dog. He was dismayed when he realized that Walter intended to let Jesse into the cab of the truck.

"I don't like to drive with a dog loose in the bed," he explained. "It distracts me and isn't safe for the dog."

So Augie found himself wedged against the window as Jesse took up most of the seat.

When they arrived at Pear Hill Park, Walter hooked Jesse to a retractable leash.

"You up for a jog?" Walter asked. "He needs to run off some steam."

"Okay."

At a moderate speed, they headed down one of the paths to the woods, Jesse loping along. Augie admired Jesse's form. With his round chest and slim back, long legs and narrow snout, the dog was built for speed. He would have liked to see him run full tilt. Not a motion was wasted.

Jesse turned his head, his tongue lolling, as if he were smiling.

When they reached a clearing, Walter slowed to a walk and let the leash out loose. It must have been twenty or thirty feet long. Then he took a worn tennis ball from a pocket and tossed it in the air. Jesse leaped after it. For the next few minutes, Jesse gleefully chased and retrieved the ball.

"You want to try?" Walter asked.

Augie took one look at the ball covered with dog slobber and shook his head. "Maybe another time."

"There's a bench at the far corner," Walter suggested. "Jesse can play while we rest."

Augie didn't mind sitting down. Louisa's vest kept him warm. Ringed by trees, the clearing was peaceful but also isolated. The sky had turned gray with a few threatening clouds, while the trees harbored darkness. If Augie had been alone, he might have been worried, but at the moment, he felt safe.

Augie glanced at Walter. He had trouble imagining him as a boy.

"Were you really beat up as a kid?" he asked.

Walter never took his eyes off Jesse. "Yup. The worst offender was Jack, my older brother."

"You have an older brother?"

Walter nodded. "Yup. A real bully when I was a kid."

Jesse lay down at Walter's feet, dropping the ball to the ground. Walter gave the dog a pat.

"We fought from the moment I could walk, and it only grew worse as we grew older."

"Wow."

Walter shook his head. "It was pretty nasty. By the time I was ten, he'd drag me behind the long barn to wallop me good. By sixth grade, he got his friends to chase me, too. The scariest time of day was just after the last bell."

Been there, Augie thought.

"When did it stop?" he asked.

"When my mother got involved," Walter said.

He leaned back on the bench and stared over the treetops, remembering.

"The summer I turned twelve, Dad put Jack and me in charge of food and water for the field workers during haying. It's hot, dusty work. We had to make sure the jugs were full and the food was out whenever workers took breaks. The trouble was that Jack was old enough to drive the tractor, and I wasn't."

Walter shook his head.

"He lorded it over me, making me fetch this and that from the house. He delivered the containers to the field without me. That ticked me off. After the second trip, Jack told me that I wasn't filling the jugs fast enough, and he said something mean about being too slow even for this job. I was so mad, I knocked him clear off his seat."

"What does this have to do with your mother?" Augie asked.

"I'm getting there," Walter said. "We had the worst fight ever. My nose was bleeding, and one of Jack's eyes had started to swell shut. Jack had me pinned to the ground and was winding up for a killer punch when Mom showed up."

"What'd she say?"

"Nothing. At least not about the fight. Her face was set like cold stone. I don't ever want to see her that angry again. She was pulling a little red wagon she used for the vegetable garden, and she announced that she needed the tractor to get to the far pasture. She left us with the wagon."

"Why'd she do that?"

"To force us to stop fighting," Walter said. "We had to take turns: one pulling the wagon full speed in front, and the other trying to prevent everything from tipping on the way. I was so tired by the end of the day, I chose sleep over supper. Jack and I didn't fight so much after that."

There was a moment of silence before Augie asked, "Why?"

Walter ran a hand through his hair.

"I'm not sure. Maybe we figured it wasn't worth it. But we learned to respect one another, and that eventually led to friendship."

"What about the kids at school?"

"They didn't stop chasing me right away," Walter admitted. "But Jack no longer egged them on—that helped. Sometimes he even told them to lay off. And it didn't hurt that I grew six inches the following year."

"I'm not about to grow six inches," Augie said.

Walter stood and looked down at Augie. "Respect comes in all sorts of ways."

Jesse jumped up as soon as Walter stood.

"Ready to go home, boy?" Walter said.

Jesse barked once and began pulling at the leash. They jogged back to the truck. After returning him to Roger, Walter drove them to a fast-food shack halfway between Pear Hill and Camden.

Augie bit into a hot dog and watched Walter as he gulped a giant soda. The man was completely at ease. Is that what happened when you earned people's respect?

"Do you ever go back to your parents' farm?" Augie asked.

"Sure," Walter said. "It's a nice place to visit."
Augie took another bite, chewed, and swallowed.
"Do you think I might get to visit?"
Walter's grin was gi-normous.
"Anytime," he said. "Any time."

The Square

WITH THE VEST ON, Augie didn't shiver once during practice. And it seemed to give him confidence—he sang with more force and depth. Even Mr. Franklin noticed.

"Excellent phrasing, Mr. Boretski."

But its bright colors worried him. They made him more of a target, he feared. Augie didn't unzip his jacket. An hour into school, Mr. Franklin sent him to his locker to remove it.

"The heating system functions well at this time of day, Mr. Boretski," he said.

When Augie returned with the vest on, the class laughed. Mr. Franklin silenced them with a glare. At lunch, Fox Tooth cornered Augie.

"Decorating for Christmas?" he said.

Dwaine arrived.

"Want to unwrap him?"

Sergio came up next.

"Let's get food," he said.

Dwaine and Fox Tooth stared at him with surprise. Sergio started to look annoyed.

"What d'ya think of the Perfessor's getup?" Fox Tooth tried.

Sergio glanced at the vest.

"It's cold during practice. I wear long johns, too."

Dwaine and Fox Tooth appeared disappointed until Sergio tugged on the vest with the tips of his fingers.

"I just keep mine on the inside," he said.

Dwaine and Fox Tooth laughed as if Sergio had scored, and to Augie's relief, they left. They hadn't even looked at his lunch bag. As he ate his sandwich, Augie puzzled over Sergio's behavior.

The following morning, the chorus was back at work.

"We have one last song to learn," Mr. Franklin said. "Mr. Boretski, please step forward."

Augie felt himself redden. He usually didn't mind being singled out during chorus. Mr. Franklin gave correction and occasional praise to everyone. Even on the days he didn't mention your name, you knew he was still paying close attention. But this was unusual.

Augie stepped forward. Mr. Franklin handed him a page of music. "By an' By" was printed at the top. Mr.

Franklin played the melody on the piano. The tune was simple. Augie hummed it to himself for a second.

"Please sing it out loud," Mr. Franklin said.

Augie sang.

"Thank you," said Mr. Franklin. "You may return to your place."

"Looks like you're gettin' a solo," Sergio whispered as Augie passed him.

Sergio's voice had an edge to it. Augie had no reply. He didn't know what was going on.

"Now, this is a spiritual," Mr. Franklin said. "We're going to make the audience remember hard times while delivering hope."

Some kids nodded as if they knew what he meant. Mr. Franklin furrowed his brow.

"The melody first," he said.

He made them run through the verses as a group. They gave a strong performance. Too strong, Augie thought. Mr. Franklin must have thought so, too.

"Very good. Now we divide up."

He took out a list and called eight names. Augie was on it. So was Sergio.

"Now we will take turns."

They sang in pairs. Verse after verse. The chorus picked up when Mr. Franklin cued them. Augie was paired with Sergio.

"No, no, no!" Mr. Franklin said. "This is a song of yearning, not a Christmas carol!"

He made them do parts over and over again. The bell rang.

"Better," Mr. Franklin pronounced, "but not good enough."

Sergio stopped Augie before they left the cafeteria. Augie noticed the dark rings under his eyes.

"Pets eat dog food," Sergio warned.

Augie understood. If Sergio thought Augie was the teacher's pet, Augie was going to be treated like a dog.

Not that he wasn't already, Augie thought. But as he walked to class, he thought about how lately Dwaine, Fox Tooth, and Sergio hadn't been treating him so badly. They didn't treat him nicely, not by a long shot, but they weren't in his face, either. They seemed almost distracted by something, so that Augie just wasn't as important. He wondered what it was and immediately decided he didn't want to know.

That afternoon, after finishing his homework in the old music room, he set out for home. Just as he rounded the corner to approach the dirty square that, in Camden, passed for a park, he saw Dwaine standing by one of the broken-down fences. Augie's heart froze. His first instinct was to double back and go around the block, but Dwaine had seen him.

"Keep movin', Perfessor," he growled.

Then Augie noticed Fox Tooth checking things out down at the other end of the square. They were lookouts, Augie realized, for the street gang who owned the park!

Technically, of course, the park belonged to the city. Maybe eons ago, it had looked like a park. But now a dirty patch of earth and gravel covered the block, with the skeleton of swings in one corner, a sorry-looking tree in the middle, and lots of broken glass and garbage everywhere. Drug dealers leaned up against the bit of chain fence that hadn't been torn down, smoked non-stop, and handed small plastic packets to passing cars for the right amount of cash. No one lived in the houses next to the park—they had been abandoned years ago and now housed homeless transients and addicts.

Augie had to walk past several buildings down the block before he reached houses in which people actually lived full-time. Augie's home was another two blocks down, in the middle of a quieter row of two- or three-story rectangular houses, sandwiched together with only the occasional alley between them. Mostly, Augie's house wasn't bothered. Mrs. Lorentushki had installed bars on all the windows. She'd lived there going on forty years and didn't see the point of leaving.

"Not for some hoodlums!" she exclaimed whenever her daughter pressed her to move.

The police periodically raided the park or the vacant buildings next to it, but the street gang replaced the arrested kids with new ones eager to make a fast buck. Being lookout was the first step, and the youngest kids were always chosen for the job.

Fox Tooth didn't show up at school the next day. That afternoon, only Dwaine stood at the corner. Augie walked on the other side of the street, but even from that distance, he saw that Dwaine seemed uneasy. One of the older kids dangling a cigarette walked over to Dwaine, and Augie sped up. The next morning Fox Tooth arrived at school with a nasty bruise along the left side of his face, darkening his dark chocolate skin into a mean shade of purple. Mr. Franklin read the note he handed to him.

"I see," Mr. Franklin said. "Your makeup homework is on your desk."

By lunchtime, even Augie had heard the rumors. Fox Tooth's mom had seen him being a lookout. When he had arrived home that night, his stepfather had been waiting. He had beaten Fox Tooth so bad, Fox Tooth didn't dare come to school the next day. His mom decided to send him down south to stay with an aunt for Christmas. He didn't know whether he was coming back.

"Tough luck," Augie overheard Sergio say.

Fox Tooth grunted.

Dwaine seemed to be avoiding Fox Tooth's eyes.

Whatever job Sergio had with the gang, he still made it to practice on time, although he looked exhausted. On Friday, he sounded hoarse.

"Take a rest, Mr. Barnaby," Mr. Franklin said. "I think you should sit out this practice."

Augie found himself singing parts on his own, searching for Sergio's voice and realizing it wasn't there. He hadn't expected to miss him!

At lunch, Augie almost walked into a heated argument between Sergio and Dwaine. Fox Tooth looked on.

"I mind my business, you mind yours," Sergio said.

"'Cause you ain't there, Fox Tooth's been kicked out," Dwaine replied.

"I don't take the blame for that," Sergio hissed.

"What kind of reinforcements are you?" Dwaine said.

"No kind—" Sergio said.

"Company," Fox Tooth interrupted.

They whirled on Augie.

"Git," Sergio said.

Augie ran.

Augie thought he should be relieved that they were squabbling amongst themselves, since that meant they weren't focusing on him. But all he felt was uneasiness.

The Horse Farm

ON SATURDAY, AUGIE MADE sure to wear his vest. Walter had promised him a trip to the horse farm.

"We'll be back late," Walter said.

"No problem," Mom said. "I'll tell Mrs. Lorentushki you'll be home after I leave for work."

The ride north had Augie nervous. He wasn't sure what to expect when they got there.

As they pulled up to a long ranch house, a woman of average height with short gray hair stepped out of the front door.

"Walter, I'm so happy you made it."

Walter grinned. The woman wrapped her arms

around him and gave him a fierce hug. When she let go, Walter introduced her.

"Augie Boretski, this is my mother, Ms. Eliza Jones."

Ms. Jones smiled down at Augie. She looked him over with a twinkling eye and extended her hand.

"I am under instructions not to pester you with questions, but I am pleased to meet you."

Walter turned red all the way to his ears, while Ms. Jones's smile could have melted an iceberg. Augie laughed. He liked Walter's mom. If she did ask questions, he'd answer them.

"I made a plate of fudge," Ms. Jones continued. "Let's not have it go to waste."

Sitting at the kitchen table with glasses of milk and a platter of fudge, Augie began to relax. Walter asked his mother about the farm, and they launched into a discussion about some construction project. Augie didn't mind.

"Where's Dad?" Walter asked.

"In town with Jack," Ms. Jones said. "He'll be back for dinner."

"Mind if we ride?" Walter said.

Ms. Jones gave another super-warm smile. "I have Merchant ready for you. What about you, Augie? Up for a tour?"

Augie hesitated. He wasn't sure about riding. He'd never done it before. But Walter looked eager, so Augie decided to try.

"Sure," he said.

The reality of riding, however, was terrifying.

First there was the size of the animal. No one had warned him that horses were so big. He had never met an animal this big before—except for the elephant he had seen at the circus, but that didn't count. The horse's head loomed way above Augie's.

"Put your left foot in the stirrup," Walter instructed.

Sure, Augie thought, except the stirrup was higher than his shoulder. He struggled to reach it with his foot, when Ms. Jones coughed. Walter gave him a boost, and he was able to swing on.

Well, sort of.

Augie landed on the saddle, facing forward no less, but the horse wasn't standing still! Augie gripped the saddle with both hands as he felt the animal shift its weight from one foot to another. Augie hadn't counted on the feel of an animal under him, breathing, moving, even if only to flick away a fly with its tail. Augie felt so unsteady. Sweat beaded on his forehead.

He was making a fool of himself.

After what felt like hours, but was probably just a minute, he was able to look up. He noticed Ms. Jones's concern.

"You okay up there?" Walter asked.

"Fine," Augie replied through his teeth.

He *would* be fine, he vowed. He wasn't going to make a total fool of himself.

Walter showed him how to hold the reins. Augie didn't want to let go of the saddle, but he pushed himself to make the effort. He gripped the horse tighter with his legs. The horse stepped forward. Augie clutched the saddle again.

"Whoa," Walter said, grabbing the bridle. "Relax, Augie," he said in a voice only Augie could hear.

"I have work to do in the back stall," Ms. Jones said, shaking her head. "We'll catch up later."

Walter nodded to her but kept his eyes on Augie.

"This is another one of my dumb ideas," he said, positioning himself to help Augie off. "I don't know why I expect people to take to horses just 'cause I grew up with them."

"Don't apologize," Augie said. This definitely was a problem he wasn't going to run away from. "Teach me how to ride."

Walter's eyebrows shot up.

"Okay."

They started in the corral. Walter mounted a white horse and led Augie's mare round and round. A few circuits later, Augie felt more comfortable with the movement of the horse, the up-and-down swaying rhythm of the saddle. This wasn't so bad. Walter handed him the reins.

"Try to follow me on your own."

Again they walked around and around. This wasn't difficult. Augie's horse followed Walter's easily. Augie hardly had to do anything.

"Now try to direct her to the gate and stop her when you get there."

Augie pulled the reins to one side—too hard, he realized, because the horse almost turned back the way she came. After a little effort, he pointed her in the right direction, then pulled hard to stop. The mare snorted.

"You're doing great. Just a little gentler, and you've got it."

Then Walter led them out. Away from the safety of the covered corral, tension started to build again. A cold breeze froze Augie's sweaty brow. But the animal under him was warm, and Augie willed himself to relax. He concentrated on Walter's back, felt the motion of the horse under him, and kept his balance at all costs.

Walter led them behind the farmhouse and up a dirt path lined on both sides with bare trees. The road opened up into a circle of four cottages.

Walter reined his horse to a halt. Augie pulled up next to him, proud of what he had accomplished. Walter motioned to the cottages.

"My mother rents these out in the summer," he said, "as a kind of artists' retreat."

Walter gave his horse a nudge, and Augie followed

him around the little buildings, now cold and empty, to a gazebo perched near the bank of a pond. He saw canoes turned over on wooden supports, covered by a tarp, and disassembled picnic tables nearby. Walter dismounted, tied his horse next to the gazebo, and helped Augie down. Augie felt relieved to touch solid ground again. Walter walked to the edge of the pond, picked up a stone, and skipped it across the surface. He gave Augie a "join me" smile. Augie did. He found skipping stones easier than when he had tried it at Pear Hill Park.

"Is this where you learned how?" Augie asked.

"Yup. Drove Mom crazy. This part of the property was off-limits when there were guests in the cabins."

Augie threw a pebble that skipped twice before it sank.

"Why was that?" Augie asked.

"To keep it quiet while the guests worked," Walter said, "or something like that."

Augie glanced at the tall man. He was grinning.

"No one complained too much," Walter added.

Augie laughed. Walter threw a last pebble in and dusted his hands on his jeans.

"Come on. I have something to show you."

Around the bend in the pond was a patch of trees, now bare. Walter pointed to one close to the water's edge. Augie stared at it but didn't see what was so interesting until they walked under it. A platform was nestled in the first fork of the trunk, about halfway up. Then Augie noticed the blocks of wood nailed into the trunk. They formed a ladder.

"Can I climb up?" Augie asked.

"Well . . ." Walter seemed a little uncertain.

"You can come, too," Augie said.

Walter shook his head. "I'm too big. We built this when I was your size."

Augie kept his eyes on the platform. He'd never been in a tree house before. He might not like boats or riding horses, but climbing was something he wasn't afraid of.

"I'll test it out," he said. "I won't step on anything unless I know it's safe."

Walter thought about it.

"Okay. But there'll be hell to pay if anything happens."

"Nothing'll happen!"

Augie climbed carefully. There were seven rungs on the ladder, and the third one had come loose. He reached up for the next one. It felt solid. At the next-to-last rung, he felt the platform.

"Where'd you get these boards?" Augie called down. "They look mighty thick."

"Found them when they rebuilt the barn," Walter said.

He sounded cagey. Had Walter stolen the boards? Augie couldn't believe it.

"Did your parents say you could use them?"

Walter laughed. "Nope. When Mom and Dad found out what we'd done, they gave Jack and me double chores for the rest of the summer. But you know," he continued, "when we came back here in the fall, we discovered that Dad had shored up the beams and added lots of straight nails to hold it solid."

"It still is," Augie said.

The wood looked darker here and there, but nothing gave. The platform didn't even creak. Augie had a great view. The bank on the other side of the pond rolled up into pastures ringed by fences. In the other direction, Augie could see past the gazebo, over the cottages, to the gray treetops of the lane they had ridden through.

"This is awesome."

"I thought so, too," Walter replied.

Augie imagined himself holed up, maybe with Louisa's book, watching a sunny day go by. But this was a gray December day, and a blast of wind across the pond made the tree sway and Augie shiver. He climbed down.

"Could we come again when it's warmer?"

"If there are no residents to disturb."

Augie stared at Walter. "*You're* going to turn me in?"

Walter raised his hands in protest and laughed again. When they returned to the house, Ms. Jones had hot chocolate waiting.

On the trip home, Walter was quieter than usual, and Augie found himself needing to fill in the quiet. He had never, ever felt the need to do that before. The silence was awkward.

"Your mom's pretty cool," Augie said.

"Oh?"

Walter steered the truck onto the highway, intent on the road. Augie felt the gusts of wind pushing against the side of the vehicle.

"She's in charge of things," Augie said. "She manages a horse farm, runs a summer camp for people, and has time to make fudge and hot chocolate, too."

Walter didn't reply. A few minutes later, the truck exited into one of the highway rest stops.

"I think I need some coffee," Walter said.

The rest stop felt dirty. The tiles on the floor were an ocher brown that looked as if they were covered in grime. The overbright fluorescent bulbs tinged everyone blue. And the brown tables with attached seats were riveted to the floor and worn pale.

Walter ordered a large black coffee and bought Augie some fries and a chocolate shake. They sat at a booth in a corner. The rest stop was almost empty, and Walter and Augie had the area to themselves.

Walter took a sip before leveling his eyes at Augie. Augie decided to concentrate on his french fries, avoiding the stare. Walter began speaking anyway.

"I think your mom is in charge, too."

Augie hadn't expected this. He looked up. Walter's gaze was friendly. Augie looked back down.

"I dunno. She's a waitress. Has been forever. She has a boss who tells her what to do. And she's stuck in Camden. What kind of *being in charge* is that?"

"Well, I can't say," Walter said.

He took another sip of coffee.

"But since you're asking . . . your mom has kept you fed and safe. She's made time to be there for you when you've needed her. She taught you how to sing—"

"I taught myself," Augie interrupted.

"If you say so," Walter replied.

Augie was getting annoyed. He hadn't expected a lecture about his mom. He liked her just fine. Walter didn't have to go on and on about it. Augie picked at the last fries in the bag while Walter sipped more of his coffee.

The gloom of the rest stop had seeped into Augie. His visit to the Joneses' farm seemed a distant memory.

"Let's go home," he said.

Walter nodded. He found one of those special covers for hot drinks and grabbed the chocolate shake.

"For the truck," he said.

Augie swung the restaurant door open for Walter just as a gale of wind whipped through. With his back holding the door, Augie zipped his jacket as high as it went and tucked his chin in. He could smell the farm in the collar. He closed his eyes for a split second.

"Come on," Walter called. "I'm freezing here."

Augie caught up. He held the drinks while Walter unlocked the cab. Augie sat, shivering but thankful, as Walter revved up the engine and set the heat to full blast. Walter cradled the cardboard coffee cup in his hands.

"A storm's blowing," he said.

Within five minutes, thin, mean rain began falling sideways. As they approached Camden, the traffic lights swung wildly. The few people they saw outside were struggling against the wind, holding on to hats and coats. A few plastic bags flew high across the road.

When they reached Augie's house, Augie noticed that one end of the string of Christmas lights had come loose and swayed in the wind. Walter walked him to the door. Mrs. Lorentushki was waiting.

"You call Mama at the diner," she told Augie. "She want to know you're home safe."

Augie nodded and started up the stairs.

"You want to stay, Mr. Jones?" Mrs. Lorentushki asked. "Be out of the weather."

"I'll make it home fine," Walter said. "Thank you."

Augie turned and saw Walter move his gaze from Mrs. Lorentushki to Augie, then back to Mrs. Lorentushki. She put her hand on Walter's arm.

"We be fine, too," she said. "I look after the boy."

Mrs. Lorentushki stood at the door as Walter leaned into the wind for the few yards to his truck. He had one hand raised in front of his face to keep out the stinging rain. Mrs. Lorentushki didn't shut the door until the truck's engine roared and Walter began to pull away. She seemed surprised to find Augie still on the stairs.

"Your mama is waiting for your call," she said.

"I'm heading up," he replied.

The wind howled around their empty apartment, rattling the windows. The lights flickered a bit when Augie spoke to Mom on the phone. Then the rain came down in earnest, pelting the roof and panes. Augie read for a while but was only too happy to snuggle under his covers that night.

As he drifted off to sleep, a small part of him noticed that he felt safe.

MARIE-LOUISE DE BOURGAILLE NORDRITCH

THE HALF-FAIRY LOUISETTE DE BOURGAILLE poured her eternal youth into her daughter, Marie-Louise. As Marie-Louise grew, Louisette withered away, so that by the time Marie-Louise turned twenty, Louisette was an old crone. She became wrinkled, blind, and bent, although her mind remained as sharp as ever. Too weak to leave her bed, Louisette summoned her daughter.

"Take the box on my desk," she said. "Use it when you need it most."

"I need it now," Marie-Louise cried, "to save you."

Louisette smiled and raised a bony hand to her daughter's face.

"I have had my time. It is as it should be."

A few days later, Louisette died in her sleep.

Overwhelmed by grief, Marie-Louise shut herself in.

Neighbors worried about the young woman and brought her food and kind words, but she barely acknowledged them. A matron from across the way came in to clean one day.

"We must open the shutters and let in some air," she said.

The first object the sunlight illuminated was the wooden box, set on a table by the window.

"How pretty," the woman said. "It looks very old."

"It belonged to my grandmother," Marie-Louise said.

The matron lifted the box and gave it to Marie-Louise.

"Then it is precious," she said.

Marie-Louise still held the box in her lap when the matron left. She smoothed the surface, feeling the warmth of the polished wood. It vibrated under her hand, as if it were humming. The hinges shimmered. Marie-Louise opened it. Inside was a stone key.

She lifted it up. It shone like metal, and the intricate stonecutting surprised her. What tools had been employed to create such a masterpiece? She turned it around and around, admiring every angle, gauging its weight, marveling at its balance. What did this key open?

She slid the key into her apron and sat back. She remained seated, transfixed, as shadows lengthened and night fell. Eventually, Marie-Louise roused herself and lit a candle.

She placed her mother's box in an armoire in her bedchamber, locking it in. It was precious, after all. Without thinking, she slipped the metal skeleton key for the armoire into the pocket of her apron, next to the stone one.

The next morning, for the first time since her mother's death, Marie-Louise felt ready to engage in the tasks of the living. She reached into her apron for the key and unlocked the armoire to find a fresh petticoat. She immediately noticed that the wooden box was no longer on the shelf! Aghast, Marie-Louise emptied the armoire, but the box wasn't there. She despaired. Her gift from her mother was lost! Tears welled up. She shut the armoire door. She turned the key to lock the door, and that is when she realized she had used the stone key.

The stone key fit the armoire! She tried it again, unlocking the door this time, and when she opened it, the box was back on the shelf, exactly where she had left it, as if it had never disappeared. She repeated this over and over, locking and unlocking, the box there and then gone, there and then gone. The perfect hiding place, Marie-Louise thought.

She left the metal key in the lock and placed the stone key on top of the armoire, behind a raised frontispiece. No one would find the stone key there. No one would look for it, not with a working key in the lock.

And though her heart was still heavy, she turned her mind to her mother's business and made it thrive. In time, her grief subsided as her life filled with her work and the people she met in the shop. Located near universities and academies for young gentlemen, the store attracted students and teachers. Perhaps absorbed by their studies or by the revolution and following wars, Marie-Louise's customers never seemed to notice how little she aged. Nearing one hundred, she looked no older than thirty.

Late one November night, a Quaker gentleman knocked at Marie-Louise's door.

"Thomas," she said, "come in out of the cold."

The elderly man shook his head.

"Thou hast been my neighbor for many years, my friend," Thomas said.

"Good neighbors," she replied.

Thomas nodded. His odd behavior confused Marie-Louise. Why did he appear so worried?

"Can I count on thy strength?" he asked.

Bewildered, Marie-Louise said, "Of course."

Thomas beckoned into the shadows. A young black woman stepped forward. She shivered in the wind and clutched an infant to her chest. Marie-Louise did not hesitate.

"Come in and find safety."

Marie-Louise knew the cruel law: an escaped slave could no longer find refuge in the North. Her legal owner might come after her. This young woman and child had to flee all the way to Canada while hiding from bounty hunters along the way.

Marie-Louise found extra bedding and blankets and fed the young mother. At daybreak, before the bustle of the city started in earnest, Marie-Louise brought mother and child to her bedchamber. Next to her armoire was a small door.

"Climb the stairs," she said. "The attic is small but warm. I will push the armoire in front of the door."

The woman nodded.

Around noon, the elderly neighbor reappeared with a Negro gentleman at his side. The young man was tall and sinewy, with walnut skin, a broad nose, and shining brown eyes. He was introduced as Emmanuel Nordritch.

"He is a trusted friend," the neighbor said, "engaged in commerce."

"What nature of commerce?" Marie-Louise asked.

"I am a conductor," Mr. Nordritch replied. "I am very good with delicate packages."

"Perhaps you could help me with a delivery," Marie-Louise said.

"I would be happy to oblige."

Close to midnight, Emmanuel Nordritch knocked twice at the back door. Marie-Louise gave the young woman a loaf of bread for the next leg of her journey and her mother's old cloak to ward away the cold. But she had nothing for the baby.

"I hold 'im close," the woman said. "He be fine."

"Wait," Marie-Louise said. "I have a flannel kerchief. You can use it to cover his head."

She searched her armoire but could not find it. Time was short. The woman had to flee. As Marie-Louise worried that she would not find it in time, she thought of the wooden box. Quickly, she locked and unlocked the armoire door with the stone key. She took down the box and opened it. Inside was a simple but warm baby bonnet fashioned out of old flannel.

"My Barnaby, he thank you," the woman said.

"Godspeed," Marie-Louise told her.

"I shall return in a few months," Emmanuel said.

"I will be waiting," Marie-Louise replied.

In the next few months, Marie-Louise cut a hole in the back of her armoire and moved it permanently in front of the doorway to her small attic. She brought up bedding and blankets, and she washed and mended old clothes for people to change into. She locked away the hiding place with her stone key.

One midnight in February, Emmanuel Nordritch knocked twice on her back door. She introduced him to a young man and woman whom she had hidden. The woman clutched a flannel shawl around her shoulders that Marie-Louise had found in her box. Emmanuel led them away.

"Godspeed," Marie-Louise told them.

"I shall return," Emmanuel said.

"I will be waiting," Marie-Louise replied.

In the next years, Marie-Louise saw Emmanuel Nordritch at uneven intervals and only at night. After handing her departing charges a last gift of soft flannel, she always gave the same heartfelt farewell.

"Godspeed."

Emmanuel always promised to return. Marie-Louise always promised to be waiting.

One sunny afternoon, Emmanuel Nordritch entered Marie-Louise's shop through the front door. He wore the uniform of the Union Army. She closed her store and heated tea. Their conversation was muted and sad. Marie-Louise had seen men return from war and had seen the horrors they carried, reflected in their eyes. And although not quite thirty, Emmanuel knew the cruelties that humans could inflict upon one another.

"I must leave," Emmanuel said.

Marie-Louise fetched her wooden box and opened it one more time. She took out a flannel kerchief, the one she had searched for, many years ago. A tear rolled down her cheek.

"Godspeed," she said.

Emmanuel used the kerchief to wipe away her tear.

"I shall return."

"I will be waiting," she replied.

Four years later, Emmanuel returned. He was gaunt,

tattered, and limping on a crutch, his black hair flecked with gray. Only his eyes had kept their youthfulness.

"I have something for you," he said.

He took out the kerchief, clean but frayed.

"It was a gift," Marie-Louise said.

Emmanuel nodded.

"Please look inside."

Within the folds of the cloth, Marie-Louise found a scrap of paper, smudged at its center. She did not understand. Emmanuel looked down as he explained.

"You gave me this kerchief and a tear upon my departure. They sustained me whenever I held them close to my heart. And when I was wounded, the kerchief stanched the flow of blood."

He turned on his crutch and looked out the shop window.

"The nurse did not know. Fevered and weak, I did not see her take the kerchief while she changed my bandages. She threw it in a pile of rags to be burned."

Emmanuel's voice strangled. Marie-Louise waited. Soon, Emmanuel pressed on.

"When I woke, a day later, I asked for the cloth. Another nurse tended me, and she did not know what had become of the kerchief. During my convalescence I despaired that I had lost it. But I found it again, a month later. It must have been dropped before it could be burned, and a ragman found it. It was too dirty for him, so he gave it to a washerwoman with some others, in exchange for her services. I saw it flapping on her line."

Emmanuel smiled ruefully as he turned to look at Marie-Louise.

"She must have thought me addled, because I broke into tears at its sight. 'If that rag means so much to you, you may have it,' she said. She refused the coin I offered. I saved one of my tears of joy on that bit of paper."

Marie-Louise lifted the scrap and put it to her cheek. Then she went to her armoire and returned with her box.

"I shall keep it here," she said, "for when it is needed most."

Soon Marie-Louise and Emmanuel were married in a tiny chapel a few blocks from the bookshop.

The world seemed to move faster around them. Discoveries, inventions, and wealthy empires grew. Yet Marie-Louise and Emmanuel established a life of calm and happy company. Emmanuel brought with him energy, good sense, and kindness. The business never flagged. And somehow, over the course of fifty years, not only Marie-Louise, but Emmanuel aged slowly. Marie-Louise appeared no older than forty, Emmanuel no more than fifty.

"Healthy habits and a life of honest work," Emmanuel explained to anyone who asked for the secret of their youthfulness.

And then, beyond all expectations, Marie-Louise became pregnant.

Turmoil roiled abroad. War drums beat, and fighting ensued. In 1917, on the day the United States declared war upon Germany, Marie-Louise delivered her one and only daughter, Louisa Nordritch. Within six months, Emmanuel Nordritch was dead, felled by influenza.

School's Closed

WHEN AUGIE WOKE THE next morning, Camden was covered with a sheet of ice. The lights were out, and Mom was making breakfast on the gas stove. The sun outside made everything glisten.

"I won't be going to work today," she announced. "I called the diner; they don't have power, either."

A large pot of water boiled on the back burner.

"What's that for?" Augie asked.

"Heat," Mom replied.

Augie borrowed one of Mom's sweatshirts and wore a shirt and his vest under it. He layered two pairs of sweatpants and socks over his legs and feet.

"I feel like a sausage!"

Mom laughed. "It's not so bad. Besides, with the sun it'll warm up, and the lights will be on soon enough."

But the temperatures never rose, and the repair crews didn't reach Augie's neighborhood until the next day. Schools throughout the city had to be closed. Late in the afternoon on the second day, Augie heard the whine of chain saws cutting fallen trees. When he went to bed, the lights still weren't on, although the temperature outside had started to rise.

He slept in his clothes. For a second night, Mom piled all of the blankets on his bed and shared it with him.

"We'll have heat tomorrow," she said.

It came on around midnight. The clanging pipes woke Augie. He set his alarm to get up for practice.

At 7:20, Augie arrived at the front door of the school. To his surprise, Ms. Cofrancesco and the custodian were there also. They were talking with Mr. Franklin, who looked dismayed.

"Pipes froze," Augie heard. "Extensive damage." "Two or three weeks to repair."

The adults stayed in a huddle while more and more chorus members waited to be let in. Kids began to grumble. The huddle broke. Mr. Franklin looked deflated. Ms. Cofrancesco addressed the crowd.

"Students! I realize that you are here to conduct practice, but I am afraid that it has to be canceled."

Murmurs rose. Someone shouted, "Like hell!" Mr. Franklin roused himself.

"Silence! Listen to what Ms. Cofrancesco has to say."

The group settled down, but Augie felt the tension.

"Thank you, Mr. Franklin," she said. She turned to the kids. "The power outage over this past weekend knocked out the heat."

"Like there was any to start with," said one of the boys.

Ms. Cofrancesco ignored him.

"The pipes froze in several places and burst. There has been serious water damage in the library, the cafeteria, and in several classrooms. Mr. Smith will need about a week to fix the pipes for heat again, and then more time to clean up and repair the damage. We will have to keep school closed until January."

There were some cheers from the crowd, but most kids were silent. Augie was trying to absorb what had been said. School was going to be closed for at least three weeks.

"What about our concert?" one of the girls asked.

"We have to cancel it," Mr. Franklin replied.

"But what about all our work?" said Fred Washington.

"Yeah," Evelyn Carbón said. "We came in early and everything."

"Your dedication is admirable," said Ms. Cofrancesco.

"I bet the Housing Authority could get the heat fixed faster than you guys," interrupted Sergio.

Ms. Cofrancesco looked pinched. Her tone became snotty.

"We are a public school, Mr. Barnaby. We have to deal with purchase orders and contractors, and other details of which you have no understanding." She tightened her coat. "You are dismissed."

She left for her car, and the chorus surrounded Mr. Franklin.

"It don't take so long." "Can we practice someplace else?" "Ms. Cofrancesco never wanted us to sing."

The custodian, who was standing off to the side, shook his head. "You know, you kids have got it wrong."

Augie turned to look at him. "What do you mean, Mr. Smith?"

"I mean she didn't tell you everything."

Sergio heard the last remark. "I knew it. She was lying to us."

"No," Mr. Smith said. "Not lying."

Mr. Smith seemed very uncomfortable. More kids were listening to him now, waiting for him to say more.

"There's no money in the budget for these kinds of repairs," he said. "Insurance money will take weeks, maybe months, but the city won't cough up if they see other money comin'."

"What does money have to do with it?" a fourth grader asked.

"No money, no repairs," Sergio said.

"But Ms. Cofrancesco said we'll have school in January," Evelyn said.

"You will," Mr. Smith said. "They'll split you up into the other schools in town. This building will be closed at least till next fall."

When Augie returned home and told Mom, she was troubled by the news.

"I wonder which school you'll end up in," she said.

Augie knew that going to another school meant busing and a whole new set of kids to deal with. Willard might not be great, but he knew where he stood.

"Do you think they'll have a chorus?" he asked.

"I don't know," Mom said. She sounded doubtful.

As Mom left for the diner, she rumpled his hair.

"Don't worry, it'll work out. Why don't you use some of your spare time to help Mrs. Lorentushki?"

He found the old lady standing in front of the porch, looking at the dangling Christmas lights and tsk-tsking.

"It's okay, Mrs. Lorentushki," Augie said. "I can put them back up."

"Too big a job now," she replied. "Look."

He saw what she was pointing at. Most of the gutter had fallen down. The weight of the ice must have been too much. The gutter had twisted and bent as it had loosened. Now only a couple of half-pulled nails held it onto the porch roof. It almost looked like a post.

"The roofer say he's busy," Mrs. Lorentushki said. "Maybe next week he fix."

Augie touched the hanging gutter. The metal was thin. It bent easily.

"How 'bout I try to fix it?" he said.

"No, no. Not a boy's job."

"Let me try. I can't make it any worse."

Mrs. Lorentushki pondered this. "Okay. But if you have trouble, you stop, and we just pull it all out for the roofer."

Augie agreed.

With Mrs. Lorentushki watching, he leaned the ladder near the bend in the gutter. Sure enough, he was able to twist it almost straight. He nailed in the two loose nails while holding up the long end of the gutter with his other hand. But when he moved the ladder to nail in the other side, he had to let go. The gutter only held for a second before twisting back down, this time with an added fold in the metal. Augie had only made it worse!

He didn't give up, though. He decided to move the ladder farther down. He figured he could climb up with the long end of the gutter, unbending it as he did so, then secure it in the middle before nailing in the ends. Unfortunately his plan didn't work. As he climbed, the gutter did unbend, but it also pulled out the two nails that he had hammered in. Before Augie reached the roof, they popped out entirely and the gutter came crashing down.

A round of applause greeted the noise. Augie looked over his shoulder and saw Sergio and Fox Tooth laughing. Mrs. Lorentushki ignored them.

"Leave it there," she said. "The roofer fix it next week."

Augie didn't want to admit defeat, especially not now with an audience.

"Since it's down, I'll untwist it first. Then I'll nail it up."

"The roofer do it," Mrs. Lorentushki repeated.

"No, I will!"

He hadn't meant to sound so forceful. Mrs. Lorentushki stood with a hand over her mouth while Augie struggled with the twisted metal. He had unfolded it but couldn't get the kink out.

"Try the hammer," Sergio called.

Augie glanced up. Sergio and Fox Tooth were still watching. Fox Tooth looked as if he hadn't seen anything funnier in his life. This only made Augie, who was already frustrated, angrier and a little bolder.

"*You* try the hammer," he snapped.

Sergio raised his eyebrows and brought both hands to his chest in mock surprise.

"*Moi?*" he said. "The Perfessor can't be talking to *me*?"

Augie, who had continued struggling with the gutter, was beyond caring whom he was addressing.

"Yeah, you. Let's see if you can get this thing straight."

"Come on," Fox Tooth laughed. "Let's find Dwaine."

"He's dissin' me," Sergio replied. "Says I can't do it."

Fox Tooth looked like he didn't believe what he had just heard. He watched Sergio push up his sleeves and scowled. "Catch up later," he said.

Sergio nodded absentmindedly. He had already grabbed the hammer and begun issuing orders.

"Put that part over this flat rock. Now hold it steady at that end."

With a couple of hammer blows the kink disappeared.

"Now you hold this end up as high as you can while I do some fancy hammerin'."

Sergio moved the ladder over and nailed in one end of the gutter while Augie and Mrs. Lorentushki, with the help of two brooms, held up the other. In a few minutes, Sergio had secured the gutter back in place.

"Now hand me those lights," he ordered.

Augie complied.

Fifteen minutes later, the lights were fastened, the ladder was put away, and Sergio was handing the hammer back to Augie.

"Now that's how it's done," Sergio said.

"Come in for hot chocolate," Mrs. Lorentushki said. "You did good work."

Sergio glanced at the street. No one was there. Fox

Tooth had left without another word. Augie wasn't sure what that meant, but Sergio didn't seem troubled.

"Okay," he told Mrs. Lorentushki.

"You're good with tools," Augie said to Sergio once they were both seated at Mrs. Lorentushki's kitchen table.

She was at the stove, stirring a pot, and Sergio had stretched his legs out, making himself comfortable.

"My old man taught me."

His curt reply had a hint of "don't ask any more questions." Augie lapsed into silence. He'd never thought of Sergio as having a family. Of course he didn't think that Sergio slept in the streets, but still, it hadn't occurred to him that there might be someone out there watching over him. Mrs. Lorentushki came to the table with steaming mugs. She had caught Sergio's words but apparently not his tone.

"He's a roofer?" she asked.

Sergio seemed embarrassed. "A carpenter."

"Good trade," she said.

Sergio mumbled, "Yeah," as if he didn't quite think so.

What was wrong with being a carpenter? Augie wondered. He wished his father had been a carpenter. Maybe then he would have stuck around.

"They'll need carpenters for the school," Augie said.

Mrs. Lorentushki shook her head. "The city don't do nothing. They put you in new school, then they don't fix at all. Save money. Leave the building to rot."

Augie hadn't thought of that—another large vacant

building in the neighborhood. Something inside of him felt empty all of a sudden.

"You really think so?" he said.

"She's right," Sergio said. "Bye-bye, Willard Elementary."

"But that's not fair!"

"Life ain't fair," Sergio said.

"We could fix it," Augie said. "We fixed the gutter."

Mrs. Lorentushki smiled. Her expression was kind. "Fixing a school is hard job. Kids can't do it. There is plumbing, and electric, and mason work."

Augie felt stubborn again, like when he had been told he should leave the gutter alone. "Sergio's father is a carpenter. And I bet other kids have parents who can do things. If we all pitched in, I bet it'd work."

Sergio laughed. "And who's going to organize this?"

Even Mrs. Lorentushki appeared incredulous. Augie sensed defeat creeping in, but he didn't want to give up yet. He sat a little straighter in his seat. Someone, he decided, was going to organize this, even if it had to be him.

A Look Inside

MOM DIDN'T LAUGH WHEN Augie told her his idea.

"Why don't you talk to Mr. Smith?" she said. "He can tell you what needs to be done."

After breakfast, Augie ran over to the school.

The building loomed dark and cold. The parking lot and playground lay empty. Augie knocked on the metal doors and yelled for Mr. Smith for at least five minutes without any luck. He circled to the back. All the doors were locked tight, and no amount of pounding brought anybody out.

Maybe Mr. Smith wasn't coming back, he thought. Maybe Augie would never find him.

As Augie returned to the front, he noticed a small

white car pulling into the side lot. Mr. Franklin. What was he doing here?

Apparently Mr. Franklin wondered the same about Augie.

"Augustus, don't you have anywhere else to go?"

"I'm looking for Mr. Smith, sir," Augie said.

"Everyone has been given leave until January," Mr. Franklin said, "although Mr. Smith will probably be in and out to secure the school." He sighed. "What a waste."

"What do you mean, sir?" Augie asked.

Mr. Franklin became grim. "I don't know what the hell they think they're doing. This school could be an asset to the neighborhood. But no. They're going to let it rot!"

Those were Mrs. Lorentushki's words. That Mr. Franklin had used them surprised Augie. After all, teachers weren't supposed to tell students when things were wrong. He was used to the bland lie every day: "Everything is fine." They'd run out of textbooks? Teachers distributed worksheets and no one was the wiser—in theory. The overhead projector broke? They did without projectors—not a word to the students, not a complaint. So what if the librarian hadn't had a new book to catalog in years? She was part-time anyway.

Mr. Franklin had just broken an unspoken rule, and Augie was unsure how to respond. His awkward silence must have brought Mr. Franklin back to his senses, because his voice had a reassuring tone when he spoke, even if the words didn't reassure Augie any.

"Well, I suppose there isn't much else to be done. Maybe they can reassign me to a music position."

Augie watched Mr. Franklin fumble with his keys, looking for the one that unlocked the front door.

"Since you're here," Mr. Franklin continued, "would you help me carry out my things?"

"Sure," Augie said.

Inside, the building was dark and quiet.

"There was some damage around the circuit breakers," Mr. Franklin said. "The electric company has to inspect before they reconnect the school."

They walked in the half-light that spilled into the hallways from classroom windows. Spooky, Augie thought. The stairwell was pitch-black. Mr. Franklin produced a flashlight.

"Follow close," he advised.

Downstairs they passed rows of lockers like dark, silent sentinels. When they reached the old music room, Mr. Franklin unlocked the door. The room looked the same as it always did, if darker. Mr. Franklin propped the flashlight on his desk and unlocked the drawers.

"I don't have much," he said, "but it'll be easier with the two of us."

Mr. Franklin took out sheet music, a few notebooks and paperbacks, some pens, and other odds and ends. He filled two plastic bags and handed one to Augie.

"That should be it," he said.

The way up wasn't as scary as the way down. Augie's eyes had adjusted, and he noticed more this time round. They had almost reached the front door before he spoke up.

"You know, Mr. Franklin, the school doesn't look so bad."

"Most of it is fine," Mr. Franklin said. "The cafeteria, however, is a disaster."

"Can I see?"

Mr. Franklin thought about it for a moment.

"I suppose."

They left the bags by the front door. Mr. Franklin was right. The cafeteria was a disaster. It looked as if water had burst into the room from two places. Mr. Smith must have mopped up whatever puddles he had found yesterday, but new ones had pooled near the stage and all around the kitchen area.

"A lot of it was ice yesterday," Mr. Franklin said. "It's thawed some."

Tiles had come up, the paneling had come loose off one wall, and the large bulletin board near the stage had fallen facedown.

"Is the piano okay?" Augie asked.

He saw it at the back of the stage, far from the worst of the damage.

"We were lucky," Mr. Franklin said. "I moved it on Friday."

Augie climbed up. He tinkled a few of the keys and thought of Mr. Franklin's brother, and his wonderful performance the Wednesday before Thanksgiving. That day seemed so long ago. The piano tuning, the music lessons—all had gone to waste.

"Couldn't we manage for a while without the cafeteria?" Augie asked.

Mr. Franklin took him to see the girls' bathroom. A large clump of ice around one of the pipes below the window was dripping into a murky puddle. Augie saw where someone—Mr. Smith, he figured—had sawn off and capped the pipe at the break. One sink had toppled to the floor. Half the tiles were up.

"Is this all from the pipes freezing?" he asked.

"Some problems have been around for a while," Mr. Franklin said. "There never was enough money to fix them. The storm just made everything worse."

Augie heard the suppressed anger in Mr. Franklin's voice.

The classroom next to the bathroom also suffered some water damage, as had the carpet in the library, a second bathroom, and one of the kindergarten rooms.

"It's just two classrooms and a couple of bathrooms," Augie said. "Couldn't they work something out?"

Mr. Franklin sighed.

"The heat hasn't been repaired yet, nor has the

place had a chance to dry out. We won't know the full extent of the damage until then."

"You're sounding like them."

Augie didn't know why he was being so bold, but he had preferred it when Mr. Franklin had been angry rather than resigned.

"I'm being realistic," Mr. Franklin said. "It's going to be expensive to fix."

As they were locking up, Mr. Smith arrived. He eyed them suspiciously.

"The place is off-limits to students," he said.

"Augustus was helping me clear out my things," Mr. Franklin said.

He looked up at the building. Windows were shining in the sunlight.

"I'm going to miss this place," he added.

Mr. Smith snorted, as if what Mr. Franklin had said was a lot of air.

"You'll teach, Mr. Franklin. It's me who's goin' to be out of a job."

"They're going to fire you?" Augie asked.

Mr. Smith nodded. "The other schools have their own custodians. An' even if they could use an extra hand, the superintendent won't pay for it."

"And if they fixed our school?" Augie persisted.

"I'd keep my job, sure."

Mr. Smith stared at Augie, as if noticing him for the

first time. He must have liked what he saw because when he spoke next, his tone was friendlier.

"Don't worry about me, kid. I'll get work. I'm skilled labor."

"Could you fix the school?"

Mr. Smith grinned. "Sure I could. It's not the skills, see—it's the time and money we don't got. One man can only do so much in one day, and we need to buy new plumbing fixtures, flooring, Sheetrock, paneling, and a whole lot of other stuff. The school hasn't got it, and the city isn't givin' it."

"What if we supplied it?" Augie said.

"You some sort of millionaire?" Mr. Smith asked.

Mr. Smith hadn't sounded mean, but his doubt did give Augie pause. Augie decided to plow ahead.

"No. But a lot of kids' parents are carpenters and stuff. If they helped, wouldn't it go faster?"

"Well, sure," Mr. Smith said. He still sounded doubtful.

"It's a nice thought, Augustus," Mr. Franklin said, "but you've forgotten the building materials."

"An' they don't come cheap," Mr. Smith added.

"It'll be more than whatever folks here can dig out of their pockets," Mr. Franklin said.

Augie felt gloom creep in. No one thought it was possible. Why should he think any different?

Supplies and Labor

AUGIE SPENT THE REST of the week in a blue funk from which nothing, not even music, roused him. His depression followed him into the weekend.

"Something's eating you," Walter said.

Augie shrugged. He didn't feel like talking about it. He nibbled at the sandwich he had ordered. He'd never eaten a Reuben before—meat, sauerkraut, melted cheese, sauce, and lots of grease. Augie thought it tasted good, but he didn't have much of an appetite.

"I'd be bummed, too, if my school were closing," Walter said.

The school closure had made the news big-time, along with scary pictures of the damage. If Augie hadn't seen the place with his own eyes, the photos would have made him think the building was on the verge of collapse.

"I'm going to miss the chorus," Augie said.

He had said what had been bothering him aloud, for the first time, and it hurt. He had trouble swallowing.

"Maybe it'll start up again at your new school," Walter said.

"They're splitting us up," Augie replied.

Walter put down his double-decker cheeseburger. "That doesn't seem right."

"They say that it's the only way to fit all the kids into the district," Augie said. "They're closing a bunch of gyms to use as classrooms."

Augie knew that the new kids would be blamed for the loss of the gyms. He dreaded entering a new school.

"Things'll be tight," Walter said.

"It's stupid," Augie replied. "It's not like all of Willard Elementary had to be shut down."

"The damage was extensive," Walter said.

"Only two classrooms," Augie said, "two bathrooms, the cafeteria, and the library."

"That's plenty."

"If they fixed the classrooms first, we could work around everything else!"

Walter raised an eyebrow. "Sounds like you've been thinking about it."

Augie had. He let everything spill out.

"Mr. Smith said that besides the plumbing stuff, the tiles are going to be the most expensive. But the classrooms have carpets, those cheap kinds. We could replace the carpets, paint the walls, and they'd be fine."

"What about the heating system?" Walter asked.

"Mr. Smith said that it wasn't damaged. He said he'll need to bleed all the radiators, but as far as he could tell there was no problem with the system."

Walter seemed impressed by Augie's knowledge. "And who's going to do the work?"

Augie hesitated for a second. "Well, Mr. Smith knows what he's doing, and Sergio's father is a carpenter. Maybe other kids' families can chip in, too."

Walter pushed his empty plate forward, dabbed his lips with his napkin, and waved to the waitress. "It's time to get some help," he said.

Augie wondered where they were going. He remained puzzled when they reached the Pear Hill Hardware Store. Roger Hoover seemed equally surprised to see them.

"I left Jesse home," Roger told Walter. "It's too cold to keep him in the run."

"We're not here for Jesse," Walter said. He pushed Augie forward. "You remember Augie Boretski."

"Of course."

Roger smiled. Augie looked down at his shoes. He didn't know why Walter had brought him here. He felt embarrassed.

"We're here on business," Walter said.

"Oh?"

"We plan on fixing Augie's school," Walter said.

Roger laughed. "I saw the news. That'll take a lot of hardware."

"We don't need it all at once," Augie muttered.

Roger glanced at Walter. "It'll be expensive."

"Labor's being donated," Walter said.

Roger tugged his ear. "So you want help with the materials."

Walter smiled. Augie caught on. If the materials and labor were donated, the city would have to repair the school. Augie stared at Roger hopefully.

"It's a whopping amount, Walter. I can't donate all of that."

"Not all of it, Roger. You heard Augie. They don't need it all at once." Then he added as an afterthought, "Maybe other businesses can chip in, too."

An idea struck Augie. "Don't you have some things that are left over that you can't sell?"

"Sure," Roger said. "I always find a few defective parts, but that won't help you fix your school."

"How about stuff that isn't defective but isn't so popular?"

"Well, I do have some faucet sets that never move."

Augie jumped in. "We'll only need three," he said.

Roger looked at Walter. "And I have two sinks with some scratches that are otherwise okay."

Augie beamed. "I'm sure they'd be great."

Roger considered Augie. "I'll need to talk to whoever is in charge of the repairs, Augie, so that I'll know exactly what you'll need." He paused for a moment. "I'm friends with Manny, the owner of a tile company. . . . He does owe me a few favors."

"Can Mr. Smith call you on Monday?" Augie said.

"That would be fine," Roger said.

Walter grinned. "Now all you've got to do is line up the labor, and we're in business."

Augie wondered if it'd be as easy as Walter made it sound.

He began searching for Sergio Sunday morning. He had spent most of his life avoiding the boy, so it felt weird trying to track him down. All Augie knew was that Sergio lived in one of the crumbling housing projects nearby.

He checked the phone book. Three Barnabys were listed but two lived on streets across town—too far to be Sergio's address. He dialed the third number and got an out-of-service recording.

"Damn," he muttered.

At least he had an address, and the phone book had a map. He found Orange Court nestled in a group of roads with similar names. He figured he shouldn't have too much trouble finding number 45. He tore the page out and grabbed his coat.

On ground level, the streets were confusing. All the

buildings in the complex had been built in the same design: two-story brick, connected in long rows. At the top corner of each row, signs had been posted: "15–24," "10–14." Augie figured they must be the building numbers, but they weren't in any particular order, and he became lost in a maze of winding streets. He passed Orange Grove and Orange Lane before he tracked down building 44–49 on Orange Court.

Although the complex was labeled "Garden Apartments" on the map, Augie didn't see any gardens. In front of each doorway was a tiny plot of bare dirt. Some folks had put up little fences or a couple of plastic whirling flowers. One resident must have tried to grow something because Augie saw withered tall grasses and weird-looking stalks. Number 44 had a baby slide so weathered that the plastic had faded to a sickly yellow. Number 45 had a torn bag of garbage out front, still encrusted with ice.

Augie couldn't find a doorbell, so he knocked. No one answered.

Sergio had to be there! Augie had decided to come around nine-thirty on the theory that it was late enough for Sergio to be awake, but early enough so that he wouldn't be out yet. Augie knocked again, this time louder.

He heard an incomprehensible yell, followed by another voice. He couldn't make out words, but the second voice sounded like Sergio's. A pair of locks unbolted. Sergio opened the door wearing baggy sweat-pants and a T-shirt, both rumpled. He wrapped an arm around himself, holding off a shiver from the cold air outside.

"Perfessor?"

"Who's there?" yelled someone from inside.

"Jus' someone I know," Sergio yelled back.

"Can I come in?" Augie asked.

Sergio didn't seem sure, but another blast of cold air must have convinced him, because he opened the door a little wider.

Augie noticed the smell first: a combination of stale cigarette smoke and something sweet bordering on sour that he couldn't place. The apartment was warm but dim. Augie's eyes had to adjust to the half-light.

He walked into a small living room. Dirty sheets and an old patchwork quilt were on the couch. The quilt looked as if it had been made out of old clothes that had outlived their use—he noticed the outline of a flannel baby bonnet at one corner. A beat-up coffee table stood on the bare wood floor. On it was an ashtray overflowing with cigarette butts.

"Whatcha here for?" Sergio asked.

"It's about fixing the school."

Sergio looked at Augie, dumbfounded, then began to laugh.

"You still goin' on 'bout that?"

"Who's that?" a gravelly voice asked.

For the first time, Augie saw the man standing in a dark doorway. As the man stepped forward, Augie realized he must be Sergio's father: he had the same long face, lanky hands, and cherry-brown complexion. But his wiry hair was shorter and flecked with gray, his face was lined, and his eyes were red and drooped like a sad hound dog's. A cigarette hung out of a corner of his mouth.

"I'm Augie Boretski," Augie said.

Mr. Barnaby's glassy eyes barely focused. "Ain't got no money for no dang church. So go on, git."

"I'm not here for a church," Augie said. "I'm here about the school."

Mr. Barnaby gave Augie a puzzled look. He shuffled into the living room, let himself fall into an old armchair, took the cigarette out of his mouth, and ground it among the many others in the ashtray. That's when Augie recognized the sweet-and-sour smell. The smell accompanied the boozers who came in for cigarettes at the bodega—a mix of alcohol and sweat. A mix that was seeping from Mr. Barnaby's pores. Augie wanted to run away. Was this the carpenter Sergio had talked about?

"School's closed," Mr. Barnaby said. "Ain't like they checked wit' me first."

"I was thinking that it doesn't have to close," Augie said.

Mr. Barnaby raised an eyebrow. But the effort almost seemed too much, because he let himself sink back into the chair and closed his eyes. Augie glanced at Sergio, who wore a mild look of disgust.

"The Perfessor here thinks we can fix it," Sergio said.

"We can," Augie said to Sergio. "Mr. Smith knows what to do, and we can get some of the materials for free. So as long as we do the work, it'll get done."

"Who says the city will let us?" Sergio asked.

Augie didn't understand what he meant. "Why wouldn't they let us? It won't cost them anything."

Sergio shrugged, then Mr. Barnaby spoke from the depths of his chair, his eyes still closed.

"The city don' want no school. That building gone, and it's one less thing screwin' up their budget."

"But they still have to give us a school," Augie said. "Isn't that the law?"

Mr. Barnaby opened his eyes. He didn't raise his head from the chair, but he was watching Augie now.

"They gonna squeeze you in here, an' squeeze you in there, an' that be it."

"They'll have to get rid of gyms, and everyone will be on top of each other. How much learning will happen then?" Augie said.

Mr. Barnaby let out a hollow laugh. He leaned forward on one arm.

"They don' give a rat's backside 'bout no learnin'."

Augie looked from Mr. Barnaby to Sergio. They couldn't be right.

"So you just want to give up?" Augie said.

Mr. Barnaby seemed taken aback by that. "Listen, kid—what's your name again?"

"Augie."

"Augie." Mr. Barnaby let it roll around his tongue. "Good name." He put his hands together. "No one said nothin' about givin' up, boy. It's that there really ain't nothin' to do."

Augie remembered something Mr. Franklin had once said and jumped forward. Mr. Barnaby looked at him with alarm.

"Wouldn't fixing the school be something good?" Augie said.

"Well, sure," Mr. Barnaby said.

"And getting people to help would be good, too, wouldn't it?"

Mr. Barnaby and Sergio exchanged glances.

"Yeah, but . . . ," Mr. Barnaby said.

"And if we get the materials for free, that's good, too, right?"

Mr. Barnaby spread his hands.

"Sure. . . ."

"Then why stop something good because something bad's gotten in the way?"

A grin spread across Mr. Barnaby's face, revealing large gaps between yellowed teeth. "You got some spirit there, little man."

He leaned back once more, but his eyes had lost

their glassy look. He rubbed his stubbled cheek a few times. "I tell you what. If you can get the city to agree, I'll help." Glancing at Sergio, Mr. Barnaby added, "We'll both help. But don' start holdin' your breath."

Augie thanked them, but on his way home, the enormity of the task sank in. He had the doubtful leadership of Mr. Smith, the promise of a small contribution of materials from Roger Hoover, and a drunk carpenter and his unwilling son—nowhere near enough to rebuild a school.

Augie needed a miracle.

THE LAST OF THE
FAIRY GODMOTHERS

THEY CALLED THE ERA "the Roaring Twenties," but my childhood was shuttered and quiet. My mother, Marie-Louise de Bourgaille Nordritch, granddaughter of the fairy Louisa, never quite recovered from the death of her husband. She became suspicious of public places, convinced that disease lurked, ready to kill me just as it had killed Emmanuel. She kept me at home, teaching me how to read and do arithmetic using books from her shop. I learned to play among the shelves, and my friends were characters from stories.

On the rare occasions when I accompanied my mother on errands, I felt shy and out of place. I was too tall for my age—gangly and awkward. On one such venture, when I was nine or ten, a merchant asked my mother, "Why doesn't your maid carry the basket?" My mother frowned, and I was puzzled. On the next trip, a lady in a huge bonnet inquired, "She a good nigger? I'm looking for a nice colored girl to do my washing. Maybe she has a sister."

I shrank behind my mother, who hissed, through gritted teeth, "Employ your own daughter."

My mother tried to soothe away the pain, but without success. All of a sudden I saw myself as the world did: I was a colored girl, and that made me everyone's servant. I avoided strangers all the more after that and accompanied my mother outside less and less.

One day, while roaming the back room that my mother used for storage, I discovered a small wooden box on a shelf in an armoire whose back was covered by boards that did not match.

The box itself was pretty. I could sense that it was old, very old. Something about its soft edges and worn wood made it feel much used. The finish sparkled. The hinges were unusual—shells, I warranted, but I could not guess from what animal.

I opened the box. Inside I found a scrap of paper, yellowed and brittle and wrinkled in its center. My mother came upon me at that moment.

"Louisa, what have you there?"

"A paper, Mother," I replied. "I found it in this old box."

My mother touched the paper with the very tips of her fingers and burst into tears.

"Your father gave this to me," she said.

This torn scrap of paper was a gift from my father?

"It is all that is left of a tear he shed in happiness."

My father cried? My mother put the scrap back into the box.

"You may look at it, but this paper is precious, so please do not take it out."

No fear, I thought. A dried tear bore no memories for me. I had often wondered about my father. My mother had talked about his bravery and kindness, but almost never about his appearance. A few days later, I returned to the box. My mother hadn't told me I couldn't.

I opened it. Next to the scrap of paper was a photograph the size of a calling card. Portrayed in hues of yellow and brown was a tall Negro man in soldier's clothes from the Civil War. He had dark short hair, a broad nose, and gentle eyes. His face seemed solemn and sad, yet handsome all the same. To me, it spoke of kindness and generosity.

"Father," I whispered.

I kept returning to this box to view the scrap of paper and the photograph. Mysteriously, the picture kept changing. Once he was in uniform, looking dirtier than before, stirring a cooking pot, surrounded by other soldiers. One photo showed the construction of a bridge of logs; another portrayed some sort of Christmas celebration. And then, terrifyingly, another showed him sitting on a chair in a bare room, so gaunt he seemed more bones than flesh, and his leg bloodied and half missing.

Almost two years passed before I gathered the courage to open the box once again. When I did, the photograph showed my mother in a long white lacy dress of the early 1900s, her hair gathered high atop her head under a tiny hat that tilted forward. Next to her sat my father, gray-haired, in a dark three-piece suit with tails and a dark tie. Improbable as it seemed to me after my years inside the shop, they sat outside, under a tree in the grass, she reading, he admiring. They looked loving and peaceful.

This was the photograph that I kept. No further ones ever appeared in the box after that, but I was content. I had met my father at last.

When I turned fourteen, adolescence surprised me. I was unprepared for blotches on my face, growing pains, and monthly cycles of cramps and dirtied rags. I felt freakish. And the building I had grown up in seemed to have shrunk, somehow. Its narrow spaces tormented me.

"I live in a prison," I told my mother.

Despite my fear of strangers, I begged to go some-where, anywhere, to explore the world beyond the shop walls. My mother relented. That summer, she sent me to upstate New York to spend time with distant cousins—my father's kin.

I was met at the Hammondsport station by Octavio, my distant cousin's son. Round-faced and jolly, his skin several shades darker than mine, he had my father's eyes! A year older than I was, he was outgoing in every way that I was introverted. We became best friends instantly. He showed me the farm, taught me how to swim, and let me ride a horse for the first time. I read him books, picking out ones that made him laugh out loud. By the end of the summer we were inseparable.

I returned home. Throughout the fall and into the spring, we wrote letters to one another. I convinced my mother to send me to our cousins' house every summer after that.

At home I remained demure and awkward. I felt uncomfortable dealing with people, even though living above the bookstore meant that I saw customers daily. So I learned how to read them, just as I had learned to read my mother's books. I might not have been comfortable talking to people, but I understood them, better sometimes than they understood themselves.

Each June, I blossomed as I took my small bags with me to the Finger Lakes. Octavio and I were in love.

The summer I was twenty-one, Octavio and I organized a small picnic. We spread an old quilt under a large oak in a far pasture. In a basket, we had packed sandwiches, fresh berries, and a cobbler Octavio's mother had prepared. The afternoon was warm and calm. Crickets buzzed. The grasses and earth smelled sweet. We talked, laughed, and then lay lazily, looking up at the branches. A few leaves had turned yellow.

"Fall's comin' soon," Octavio said.

I rolled over and pretended to search for something in the grass.

"You will be starting law school," I said.

Octavio rolled next to me, searching the grass, too.

"Right in the city."

"Do you know where you will stay?" I asked.

"Not yet," he said. "Someplace near the university, I guess."

I tilted my head. Octavio was smiling at the grass.

"You will be close enough to visit me," I said.

"I don't want to visit you."

I gathered my knees under my skirt. The day seemed less vivid all of a sudden. A grayness was closing in at the edges.

Octavio sat up, too, so close our shoulders touched. I stared down at my feet. He stroked my face with the back of his hand, and I turned my cheek into it, smelling the earth in his fingers. A pain clutched my heart.

"Marry me," he whispered.

Tears stung my eyes. I blinked them away. This was ridiculous. I was too happy. I took his hand from my cheek, holding it in both of mine, and looked him straight in the eyes.

"I will," I said.

Octavio's parents agreed. When my mother was told, she seemed anxious.

"It's a permanent step," she warned.

"My heart is set," I replied.

Sadness filled my mother's eyes, yet her smile was genuine.

"Then no one can hold you back."

We were married Thanksgiving Day. I moved into Octavio's student flat, not too far from my mother's shop. I continued to work with her, but she insisted on paying me wages.

"I am your daughter," I protested.

"You are no longer my charge," my mother replied.

The small income proved useful in the lean years of Octavio's student life. Upon graduation, he found a position as a junior associate in a law firm led by two Negro attorneys. "Until I am on my feet," he explained. "Then I can open my own practice." A few months later, Japanese forces attacked Pearl Harbor. Not too long after, Octavio received his notice from the draft board.

"I must serve," he told me.

After Octavio went to war, my life narrowed. I moved back in with my mother to save money and for companionship. Although I volunteered at a nearby hospital, I was relegated to the laundry room. This suited me. I was still shy in public and kept to myself. I behaved as if a spectator, watching the world from a window.

Late in the war, I received the news of Octavio's death in the South Pacific. I had been fearing his death all along. In numb shock, I closed my shutters to the outside world.

My mother tried to rouse me, but I did not respond. My life was over. It had lost all its meaning. I sat in my room, the black, heavy curtains blotting out all light. I ate only rarely. Darkness enveloped me. There was no day.

Half a year passed this way. One morning my mother came up, breakfast tray in hand.

"Japan surrendered," she announced. "It's time to take down the curtains."

Daylight stung my eyes. I recoiled into a shadow, but my mother went about as if she hadn't noticed. Next to me was the tray. I stared at it. It held the usual: a glass with water, a piece of toast, a poached egg. But there was something rectangular there, too. I reached for it. A book! I hadn't touched one in so long.

I picked it up and turned it over, surprised at its weight. I stroked the rough cover while my mother finished gathering the curtains. Before she carried them away, she kissed me on the forehead.

"Nourish yourself," she said.

Without thinking, I opened the volume.

When my mother returned a few hours hence, she found the toast and egg untouched. But I was curled up on my rocking chair near the window, reading intently.

With every meal that my mother brought came another volume. I devoured the words. Not a bit of food crossed my lips, yet the gauntness around my eyes filled. Soon the grayness left my cheeks, and my hair became fuller and less brittle. After a few months of this diet, my mother appeared with the tray but without the book.

"My stories," I said.

"The wooden box is empty," my mother replied. "But many more books are downstairs, waiting."

And so I returned to the shop. At first I simply read in a far corner. But little by little, I helped my mother with this or that. One afternoon my mother asked me to take charge of the cash register.

"I must run an errand a few blocks away. I will return in an hour."

I positioned myself on the stool and smiled automatically to customers who presented their selections.

"Do you have books on birds?" a man asked.

I brought him down the aisle of science and nature books.

"Is the owner around?" a white woman said.

"I am her daughter. How can I help you?"

The woman looked at me askance—my complexion too dark for her comfort, it seemed. I braced for the old shudder of fear from my childhood, the one that always made me want to disappear. But I remained calm. She could do me no harm, I realized.

"I am looking for something for my grandson," she said, still frowning.

"How old is he?" I heard myself ask.

I sold the woman a fine edition of *The Adventures of Tom Sawyer*. She was smiling when she left the shop.

I did not notice my mother's return.

In the days that followed, I discovered that I no longer felt shy, as if the darkness I had cocooned myself in had metamorphosed me into something else. I had always been able to read people, and now I used this skill to nurture customers and make friends. I remained retiring but was engaged in life. My mother had found an heir to her business. I had found my center.

Over the years, I remained youthful, as my mother had before me. Some tried to convince me to go out and meet young men, but my mother never suggested it. She knew that I will never again fall in love. I gave my love to Octavio, and my love for him will last for all eternity.

Shedding the Donkey Skin

MOM BALKED WHEN AUGIE asked for the train fare.

"Walter can take you next Saturday," she said.

"Please, Mom," Augie begged, "it's important."

"The book isn't going to disappear. Why can't it wait?"

Augie had finished the green book and wanted to return it, but of course it was more than that. How could Augie explain? Only Louisa could help. She was the closest thing he had to a fairy godmother. Mom was looking at him suspiciously.

"The store . . ." Augie paused, trying to gather his thoughts. "It's almost magical. And I want to talk to Louisa. You know how special she is."

Mom gave a grudging nod. She liked Louisa, a lot.

"I promise I'll be home before dark," Augie continued, "and I won't get into any trouble."

Mom's mouth was twisted into a half frown, but she was listening. One last push, Augie thought.

"I almost never ask you for anything extra," he said.

This was true. He knew they couldn't afford treats, so he never asked.

Mom sighed. Augie knew he'd won. He felt a little bad about making her feel guilty.

"I can only afford to give you the train fare," she said. "No more."

Augie nodded.

"And you can't expect any more favors like this anytime soon."

Augie nodded again.

Mom took the money out of her purse. "I'll tell Mrs. Lorentushki to look out for you."

Augie gave Mom a giant hug and ran all the way to the train station. When he arrived at the bookstore, Louisa greeted him with mild surprise.

"You are alone today."

Augie nodded. He climbed onto the extra stool and placed the book in front of him.

"You finished it," she said.

Augie nodded again. She reached over and flipped through the pages. Augie caught sight of the front page that showed the picture he had seen the very first time he had opened the book—the donkey pooping gold into a dish.

"Louisa?" Augie asked.

She looked up.

"Why did you want me to read it?"

Louisa smiled, gently. "It chose you."

Augie frowned. Another one of Louisa's riddles, this one no easier to figure out than the others.

"But . . ." Augie wasn't sure how to frame the question. It seemed so nosy. But Louisa stood there, unperturbed. She waited, smile still in place, expectant but not impatient. Augie looked down at his hands.

"The stories . . . ," he said, unable to finish, again.

"Yes. They're stories," Louisa said.

"You said they were true."

Louisa nodded. Augie felt embarrassed.

"And they're about you. You and your family."

Louisa's chin tilted down, as if she were giving him half a nod. Perhaps, she seemed to be saying. Augie lapsed into silence.

In Camden, everything had been so clear. He'd run to Philly, talk to Louisa, and his problems would be solved. But now that the woman stood across from him, all his courage failed.

Louisa did not press. Customers bustled in and out that Sunday afternoon, and she answered questions and rung up sales. A man inquired about a book. She walked him to a shelf and left him there to peruse the selection. When she returned, Augie knew he had to speak or he'd burst.

"Can you grant wishes?" he asked.

He noticed a sadness in her eyes that he did not understand.

"I can't perform magic," she said.

"What about your box?"

Louisa stared at him for a moment. "What is it that you're looking for?" she asked.

"I'm not sure," he admitted.

Louisa let concern pour out of her eyes. She remained silent, but Augie felt the tug of her openness. He began to speak. He told her about the school closing, the end of the chorus, how he didn't want to be sent off somewhere else to deal with new problems and lose the bit of good that he had. How hard he had worked trying to convince people that the school could be saved, but how little they seemed to believe that it could be done. And he kept talking, voicing feelings of frustration and loss, fear and pain, telling her things he had never said aloud to anyone.

"I wish there was someone to help me," he said, "someone I could rely on. Mom has to work. Walter's just a Big Brother. What I need is a dad."

Augie hadn't expected to say that. But as the words fell out, he realized they were true. He told Louisa of his visit to Sergio's and how Mr. Barnaby was a drunk.

"But, you know," he said, "he was there. And I could

see that he cared about Sergio. And he'd help. Even if he wasn't perfect. Just like a father should. Why can't I have a little of that?"

He fell silent, overwhelmed. Tears crept up when he hadn't meant them to. He breathed deeply, trying to regain his composure.

"Do you really want to trade places with Sergio?" Louisa asked after a while.

Augie looked at his hands, again. Did he? he wondered. He thought of his home and of Sergio's stale apartment. He thought of Mr. Barnaby's rheumy eyes, disheveled appearance, and sour skin. And he thought of his mom, worried about whether he'd be home before dark. He looked up at Louisa.

"No," he admitted. "But why'd my dad have to disappear? Why doesn't he call even once in a while?"

"I can't answer that," Louisa said. "Only he'd be able to answer those questions."

"Then why don't you look in that box of yours? Maybe you can find him for me."

"I cannot give you your father," Louisa said. "No one can."

"The fairy Louisa could've," Augie said. "She gave the princess a prince."

"That's a fairy tale," Louisa said.

"You said the stories were true!"

Augie wiped away a tear. Why had he come? Louisa put a hand on his shoulder.

"Louisa gave Annette shelter and love when someone wanted to hurt her. Isn't there truth in that kind of a story?"

Augie pushed her hand away. "It doesn't give me a father."

"It did not give Annette one, either."

Augie paused at that, letting her words sink in.

"From where I am sitting," Louisa continued, "I see a lot of people trying to give you more."

At that moment, the customer returned with two books in his hand.

"I'll take these," the man said.

Augie watched Louisa ring up the sale as the man talked about some edition or another of a book. But Augie wasn't paying attention. What Louisa had said surprised him. What could be more than giving him his father? He was still thinking hard when the tinkling of the door bells made him realize that he was alone at the counter with Louisa again.

"I think," she said, "that if you have a little faith, you will succeed."

"You really think so?"

Louisa nodded. "Look at how much you have already accomplished. Perhaps it is time you shed the rest of the donkey skin."

On the train ride home, Augie wondered what Louisa had meant.

The Chorus
Gets to Work

LOUISA'S ENCOURAGEMENT HEARTENED AUGIE. There might be no castles in his neighborhood, but this was his home. He'd do what he could to keep it whole.

Monday morning, Augie went searching for Mr. Smith. He found him talking to Ms. Cofrancesco at the school. She wasn't happy to see a student arrive.

"The school is closed," she said.

"I know," Augie said, "but I need to speak with you."

He was going to say "to speak with Mr. Smith" but realized he needed Ms. Cofrancesco's help, too. He had to convince her that the school was worth saving. Otherwise how was he going to convince the city?

Ms. Cofrancesco proved less hard to convince than

he had expected. She listened patiently as Augie explained how repairs could be done.

"It's a nice plan," she said, "but the city has already made its decision."

"It won't cost them anything," Augie said.

"The city doesn't see it that way. Fitting Willard kids into other schools will be cheaper than keeping this relic open."

"But it's not just a building," Augie said. "It's kids, and teachers, and learning."

Ms. Cofrancesco's smile was sincere. "You sound a lot like Arthur Franklin." She pitched her voice deep. *"You're breaking up the community.* And you're both right. But I've been trying to tell that to the city for the last week, and they haven't listened yet."

"What if kids told them, too?" Augie said.

"Which kids?" Ms. Cofrancesco asked.

Augie was thinking quickly. There was one group of kids he knew who worked together and cared about the school.

"How about the Junior Chorus?"

Ms. Cofrancesco stared at him for a second, her eyebrows slightly furrowed.

"That is a thought," she said.

"They can practice in the gym," Mr. Smith said. "I can get the furnace up an' goin' by this afternoon."

Ms. Cofrancesco nodded. Augie held his breath, not daring to believe it.

"I'll call Arthur Franklin," she said.

She turned to Augie.

"There's a Board of Education meeting Friday evening. Do you think you can be ready by then?"

"You bet!" Augie said.

At eight-thirty a.m. on Tuesday, Mr. Franklin and the chorus were gathered in the school gymnasium. Almost all the kids had come—even Sergio! The place was piping hot, just as Mr. Smith had promised.

"We have four days to prepare," Mr. Franklin announced. "We must show this city that Willard Elementary is more than dirty walls and beat-up tiles. We must show them that we are people. We're the ones who hold it together, and we want to stay together!"

"Yeah!" the kids cried.

Mr. Franklin worked them hard. They spent the morning reviewing the songs and rehashing the arrangements. In the afternoon, Mr. Franklin concentrated on their last song, "By an' By."

"Rest tonight," Mr. Franklin said. "Don't sing. Don't talk unless you have to. Drink plenty of fluids. Gargle with salt water before going to bed. I'll see you tomorrow at eight-thirty sharp."

Augie didn't know what the other kids were doing, but even if his voice wasn't singing, his mind was. He kept going over the tunes, worrying about this phrasing and that breath. He dreamed that he was standing in the wrecked cafeteria, trying to remember the words to a song he had forgotten, all the chorus members staring at him with disapproval. Mr. Franklin was wearing a three-piece black suit with tails and a white bow tie, tapping a baton on a music stand.

" 'Mary Had a Little Lamb,' " Mr. Franklin said. "I'd expect that you'd know that, Mr. Boretski."

Augie woke in tangled sheets, barely able to move.

The kids were buzzing when Augie arrived at school on Wednesday. Most had spoken to their parents, or uncles, or aunts, or grandparents, about what was going on.

"My cousin's an electrician," Fred Washington said. "He said he'd help if we want."

"My aunt works for a tile company," Evelyn Carbón added. "She says she can take a day to help lay stuff down."

Ms. Cofrancesco, who had come in to see how things were going, took down names and phone numbers. She seemed excited, too. Sergio gave Augie an amused expression. Augie's mood soared. Mr. Franklin made them work twice as hard.

"Synchronize," he yelled. "Mr. Lapati, you are off by an eighth!"

He added a few hand movements.

"We stand in place," he said. "We don't have time to learn choreography."

At the end of the day, he handed each kid a sheet that listed clothes for girls and boys.

"You must each look your best," Mr. Franklin said. "If you don't have black pants and a white shirt, blue and white will do. If you don't own a white shirt, a light color will be fine. No logos, no pictures, no patterns. For contrast, I would like each of you to find something red to wear: a ribbon, a hat, a scarf, a tie, a plastic flower, a jacket, anything. The brighter the red the better. For those of you who do not have anything red to wear, I will bring some red items that you may borrow."

The kids sounded excited as they left the school. Augie wondered if his old black pants still fit him. He'd check to see if his vest was reversible.

On Thursday, Mr. Franklin made them run through their songs in order, still correcting them at every opportunity: "Mr. Cody, more solemnity here." "Mr. Washington, stand straighter."

Everyone was intent. Augie couldn't imagine they'd be ready by Friday evening, but they gave it all they had.

"Dress rehearsal tomorrow morning," Mr. Franklin said. "We'll take the afternoon off."

Friday morning, Mr. Franklin showed up with a box of red items: a plastic carnation, two pairs of suspenders, a handkerchief, and a roll of Christmas ribbon. For the next fifteen minutes, he made sure everyone was outfitted correctly. The chorus ran through their performance without interruption, then Mr. Franklin had them go over parts that had sounded weak to him.

"We meet at City Hall," he told them at the end of the morning. "Keep your performance clothes clean."

Sergio walked out with Augie.

"Not bad, Perfessor," he said.

Augie wasn't sure if Sergio was referring to his clothes, to Augie's singing, or to the fact that they were doing something that might save the school. It didn't really matter.

"Thanks," Augie replied.

Dwaine was standing outside, waiting for them.

"Got a new bro?" he asked Sergio.

Sergio shrugged. "Just another singer in the chorus."

"Like you."

Dwaine had said it mean. This was a put-down, but Sergio seemed determined to ignore the dig.

"Singing's fine," he replied.

"Can't be that fine," Dwaine said. "You're no star."

Sergio bristled. "I shine!"

"Like the bumper on a Chevy," Dwaine chortled.

Sergio narrowed his eyes. "At least I'm drivin' somethin'."

Dwaine pulled his mouth out like a grin. But his eyes were cold. What had happened between them? Augie wondered. At that moment, Mr. Franklin stepped out of the school, his arms laden with music sheets.

"Mr. Barnaby, Mr. Boretski," he called. "Could you please help me load these?"

"I'd say you's the one bein' driven," Dwaine said before turning on his heels and leaving.

Augie and Sergio carried music sheets and the box of red knickknacks to Mr. Franklin's car. Sergio appeared sullen. Augie felt like he had to say something. Dwaine was wrong. Sergio did shine.

"The chorus thinks you're star material," Augie said as Mr. Franklin drove away.

"Yeah. See ya later, Perfessor."

Augie watched Sergio walk in the direction Dwaine had gone.

Sergio, Down

AUGIE FOLLOWED SERGIO, ALTHOUGH he wasn't sure why. He'd always avoided trouble, and here he was, headed straight for it. He stayed at least a block behind— Sergio was easy to follow with his bright red hat perched on his head. He went straight to the park.

Augie hid in a shadow across the street, behind several trash cans. If Sergio knew he was there, he hadn't let on. Dwaine and Fox Tooth were waiting at the corner.

"If it ain't the cleaning lady," Dwaine called out.

Some of the dealers farther down the park turned their heads to see what was happening. They saw Sergio and turned back to each other. He was just another kid, nothing to worry about.

"Where's the mop?" Fox Tooth said.

What were they talking about? Augie wondered. He saw Sergio ball up his fists and say something Augie couldn't make out. Dwaine sneered and Fox Tooth giggled.

"He says he ain't no cleaning lady," Fox Tooth said to Dwaine.

"Well, someone's got to clean up after that low-down father of his," Dwaine said even louder.

Augie missed the windup, but Sergio's punch flattened Dwaine. Sergio stood over the large boy, his shoulders back.

"You're lower than the bucket he pisses in," Sergio said.

The dealers were paying attention now. One of their own had been hit, and Sergio wasn't backing down. Fox Tooth stood in shocked disbelief.

"Get him!" Dwaine screamed from the ground.

Fox Tooth tried to tackle him, but Sergio stepped aside. That's when Dwaine tripped him. Sergio fell. Fox Tooth wheeled around, and several of the dealers began heading in their direction.

Augie decided to run. He needed reinforcements.

He ran two blocks to the Garden Apartments and remembered how to get to Orange Court. Within a minute he was pounding on number 45.

"Mr. Barnaby, Mr. Barnaby!" he shouted. "Sergio's in trouble. Come quick."

Mr. Barnaby opened the door. Although he was disheveled, his eyes weren't as red as the last time. He must have caught Augie's tone if not his words, because he was alert.

"Tell me quick."

"The drug gang at the park. They're beating him up."

Augie had not expected the man to move so fast. Augie had to run to catch him.

"Ask the neighbor to call the police," Mr. Barnaby said. "She lets me use her phone."

Augie hesitated. He wanted to follow Mr. Barnaby and help Sergio. Mr. Barnaby stopped just long enough to yell, "Go!"

The elderly lady next door took several minutes before she understood what was going on.

"Li'l Sergio, he be hit?" she said.

Augie nodded. She reached for the phone.

"Them poh-lice ain' gon' to do nothin'. I'ma call my son Lucas."

"But Mr. Barnaby said—"

"Listen, chile. I knows what I'm doin'."

The neighbor punched in the numbers.

"Lucas," she said into the phone. "Li'l Sergio Barnaby need help at the square." She "Uh-hum"-ed into the receiver a few times and hung up.

"I'ma get my coat," she said. "You walk me there."

She walked slowly, with a cane.

"Nothin' but badness since them drugs come aroun'," she said on the way. "Use to be you could pull yo'self out of this mess."

By the time they reached the park, two large African American men Augie had never seen before stood next to Mr. Barnaby. He crouched at the side of another figure—Sergio, Augie thought. Dwaine, Fox Tooth, and the drug dealers were nowhere to be seen.

"You go home now, chile," the neighbor told Augie.

"But Sergio—"

"He be in good hands now. This ain' yo' business."

Augie wanted to stay, but the two men were eyeing him suspiciously. The old woman patted his shoulder.

"It all be oh-kay, now. Go home."

Reluctantly, Augie left. He saw the darker of the two large men walk over to the old lady and gently take her by the elbow. That must be Lucas, he thought. He didn't see Sergio move.

At the Board of Education

AUGIE WAS QUIET ON the ride to City Hall. Mrs. Lorentushki sat in front, next to Mom. She had insisted on coming.

"I always like a concert," Mrs. Lorentushki had said.

Augie was worried about Sergio. Was he okay?

The meeting room was packed when they arrived. The Board of Education sat on a dais, looking down at the crowd. The Board members seemed surprised by the attention. Someone had notified a local TV station, and a reporter stood in a corner, sipping from a paper cup, talking to a man holding a large portable camera on his shoulder.

Mr. Franklin herded the chorus members to one

side. Everyone was there but Sergio. Augie watched the large double doors through which people were still streaming. He saw Walter walk in with Roger. Augie waved. They waved back before wedging themselves onto a bench a few rows behind Mom and Mrs. Lorentushki. Augie noticed Mr. Barnaby's neighbor and her son Lucas seated not far from them. This gave him hope, somehow.

The large round clock on the side wall showed 7:40, but the room still buzzed with people talking, others walking in. The place felt chaotic to Augie, a jumble of noise and motion. How were they to perform? When were they to perform?

And was Sergio going to make it?

At about seven-forty-five, Augie heard sharp rapping at the front of the room. A small black woman sitting at the center of the dais banged a gavel.

"Order," she yelled, "order!"

There was a general settling down.

"We have a last-minute addition to tonight's agenda," the woman announced. "Ms. Cofrancesco, principal of Willard Elementary School, wishes to make a presentation to the Board."

From a seat at the far end of the dais, a skinny white man with wire-rim glasses interrupted the woman. His voice registered annoyance.

"Haven't we already closed matters on that school?"

"Hear her out," someone yelled from the crowd.

The gavel came down hard with another bang.

"Order!" the woman yelled.

The noise subsided into a gentle murmuring. The woman swept her gaze around before addressing the skinny man in the corner. Augie thought she acted a lot like Mr. Franklin.

"Indeed, we did close matters. But there is some feeling that not all has been said."

Ms. Cofrancesco, who had risen at the first mention of her name, was nodding. Augie noticed that she wore a red-black-and-white-checkered suit. He glanced at Mr. Franklin, who was watching, impassively. He was dressed in a black suit, white shirt, and red tie. A red carnation was pinned to his lapel.

"Ms. Chairwoman," Ms. Cofrancesco said, "thank you for your indulgence."

The woman on the dais nodded. Augie wondered whether it would hurt her if she smiled.

"Ms. Chairwoman," Ms. Cofrancesco repeated, "and members of the Board, we understand you decided to close Willard Elementary School because of the cost of repairs."

Disapproving murmurs ran through the crowd. The TV reporter, as if waking up, ordered the camera lights on, and Ms. Cofrancesco stood out even more.

"We think this is a grave mistake," Ms. Cofrancesco continued. "The school does need repair, but its students still view it as the center of their activities. You close the school, and you lose one of the foundations of this community."

The room echoed with shouts of "Yeah!" "You tell it, sister!" "The lady's right!" and "Amen!"

The gavel pounded again.

"We laud your dedication, Ms. Cofrancesco," the Chairwoman said, "but we have already met on the subject, and the decision was final."

"I don't think you have heard from all of us," Ms. Cofrancesco said. She motioned to Mr. Franklin, who stepped forward. "This is Mr. Arthur Franklin. He teaches sixth grade. He will demonstrate what can be accomplished by the students of this school if effort is applied, and people are willing."

Mr. Franklin turned to the chorus. Not a word was needed. They stood to attention. He was raising his right hand slowly when a commotion at the front door interrupted him. Mr. Barnaby entered, pushing Sergio in front of him.

Bruises ringed Sergio's eyes, both hands were bandaged, and his jacket was torn. The black pants that had looked crisp that morning were covered with mud. And he had lost the red hat.

"Sorry to interrupt," Mr. Barnaby said. "I hope we ain't too late."

Sergio looked down sheepishly as his father led him to Mr. Franklin.

"Not at all," Mr. Franklin said in a soft baritone.

Then, much to Augie's, and, he guessed, everyone else's surprise, Mr. Franklin took the carnation off his lapel and handed it to Sergio.

"You may take off your jacket," he told the boy.

Sergio looked up. For a second, Augie thought Sergio might cry, but instead he grinned and took off his jacket. He stuck the flower in a buttonhole of his shirt.

"Now," Mr. Franklin said.

Sergio quickly took his place in the chorus, and they began to sing. A mild echo bounced around the large room, and Mr. Franklin slowed the chorus's tempo a hair to compensate. One or two of the weaker singers became confused at first, but Augie and Sergio caught on immediately and helped the chorus members keep time. They sang a cheerful carol, and the crowd clapped and hooted at the end of it.

The next song, an old English tune, was quieter, but the sopranos were beautiful, and Augie could tell Mr. Franklin was pleased. Then came a rousing three-part round that the chorus executed with precision. The crowd loved it.

"Ladies and gentlemen," Mr. Franklin told the Board and the audience, "I have had the privilege of working with your children. The time they took to prepare for this was all their own. Their hard work and discipline should be an example to all of us."

The crowd applauded. The Board members nodded. Mr. Franklin continued.

"As you listen to the last piece they shall sing tonight, please consider: if they can do this, can't you do more for them?"

He turned to the chorus and pointed to Sergio and Augie. The boys stepped forward.

"Oh, by an' by."

Fred Washington and Jamil March stepped forward.

"By an' by."

The chorus jumped in.

"I'm goin' to lay down this heavy load."

Pause. The music floated into every corner of the room. Evelyn Carbón and Annie Zola stepped forward.

"Oh, by an' by."

Two more chorus members came forward.

"By an' by."

The whole chorus joined in.

"I'm goin' to lay down my heavy load."

They let the music sink into the silent crowd.

A pair of singers stepped forward again, and the entire chorus replied. Calls of hope were answered by swells of desire. The music carried the singers while Mr. Franklin kept tight control over the execution. Like the tide coming in, each verse seemed to be more powerful. In each beat of silence, the audience held its breath, waiting for the next wave to sweep in and overwhelm them. Sergio and Augie sang again.

"Oh, when I get to heaven for a sing an' shout . . ."

Chorus.

"I'm goin' to lay down my heavy load."

Evelyn and Annie replied.

"There's nobody there to throw me out."

Chorus.

"I'm goin' to lay down this heavy load."

The full chorus launched into the last refrain. And when the very last hum and that hum's very last echo had trailed into quiet, the room erupted. People were standing, cheering, stomping, clapping. Augie caught a glimpse of Mrs. Lorentushki wiping her eyes with a tissue and his mother beaming. Walter clapped, grinning from ear to ear. Augie felt full and proud, as if he had grown six inches and he had become aware of it, just now.

The gavel came down hard.

"Order! Order!"

The crowd quieted slowly.

"Order!" the Chairwoman bellowed.

Ms. Cofrancesco stepped forward.

"Thank you, students, Mr. Franklin," she said. "And thank you, parents and families, for supporting their hard work."

More cheering ensued. For the briefest second, Augie thought the Chairwoman looked uncomfortable up on the dais before she started banging her gavel again. The other Board members seemed to be admiring their hands.

"Now, Ms. Chairwoman and members of the Board," Ms. Cofrancesco said. The crowd hushed. "As you can see there is a great deal more to Willard Elementary than you have considered."

"We are very impressed by the performance," the Chairwoman said, "but school spirit does not substitute for dollars."

"I might have agreed with you once," Ms. Cofrancesco replied, "but I have been shown otherwise."

She took out a piece of paper from her jacket pocket and unfolded it.

"I have here a list of materials donated by businesses throughout the area for the school, and"—she pulled out a second sheet—"a list of parents and family volunteers who have contacted me, ready to donate their labor to repair the damage."

Cheers interrupted her. The TV reporter zoomed over to the front of the room.

"These developments tonight have caught even the Board members by surprise . . . ," Augie heard the reporter yell into the microphone.

The gavel began pounding again.

"Order! Order!"

Not Taking "No"
for an Answer

AUGIE WATCHED THE EVENING news with his mom.

"The School Board refused to repair Willard Elementary," the reporter said, "despite a spirited performance by students."

The station showed an eight-second clip of the chorus singing.

"Parents have vowed not to take this lying down."

The screen switched to a shot of Mr. Barnaby.

"Our kids and this neighborhood *deserve* their own school."

The School Board Chairwoman commented next.

"We have the best interests of the children in mind."

Behind her, Augie heard a parent yelling, "Since when?"

The local paper ran a piece the following morning under the headline: "School to Stay Closed: Board Turns Down Free Supplies and Labor." A smaller headline underneath read: "Willard Chorus Brings Spirit to Blighted Neighborhood."

"You did your best," Mom told Augie. "You can't ask for more than that."

Augie felt betrayed. The chorus, Mr. Franklin, even Ms. Cofrancesco had worked so hard, yet the School Board had refused to reopen Willard. It wasn't right.

Walter thumped Augie on the back when he came to pick him up.

"You were terrific," he said.

Augie shied away. "The School Board didn't budge."

Walter's eyes twinkled. "Don't give up hope yet."

The next day, the paper published a two-page spread about the school. Ms. Cofrancesco and Mr. Smith had been interviewed.

"The School Board, I am sure, has good reasons for its decision," Ms. Cofrancesco was quoted as saying. "I feel bad going back to the volunteers and telling them their services aren't wanted."

"It's straight plumbing and carpentry," Mr. Smith was reported saying. "With the supplies being offered, we could get it done."

Floor plans took up a portion of one page. The exact

spots where the repairs were needed were highlighted in pink. The areas looked tiny compared to the whole building.

Augie listened to a call-in show on the radio the following day and more news reports on TV. The story was being picked up and growing. Even at the bodega, where Augie went to buy some milk for Mom, people were talking about what had happened.

"We elect the School Board," one man said. "They should listen to us."

"Something should be done about them," a woman replied.

The rumblings didn't let up through Christmas and New Year's. Walter told Augie that Roger's friend the tile man was friends with the governor.

"Something's got to give," he said.

Another School Board meeting was scheduled for seven-thirty p.m. on January third.

"Better get dressed," Mom told Augie. "It's cold out."

"Where are we going?"

"To the Board meeting, of course."

Augie was mystified.

"What for? The chorus isn't singing tonight."

Mom laughed. "There might be another kind of singing going on."

Augie was surprised to see Walter and Roger there, too.

The crowd at this meeting was even larger than the last one. It was angrier, too. Augie counted three TV cameras and several other people talking into recorders. The clock ticked past 7:30. Past 7:40. And the crowd grew louder. At 7:45, someone yelled: "Let's save the school!" A chorus of cheers followed. At 7:50, the Chairwoman came out looking pinched. By 7:55, the audience roared with delight: repairs were going forward. Augie couldn't believe his ears.

Walter later told him that the supplies had been shipped that morning. He grinned.

"Some people won't take 'no' for an answer."

As far as Augie was concerned, this was proof that magic existed, even in Camden.

School didn't open on time, though. Two weeks passed before the classrooms were fit enough for students to return. The repairs on the cafeteria took the longest. Mom talked to her boss, and he agreed to work out a deal to deliver food. Kids ate at their desks for a month.

Some things didn't change. Mr. Franklin convened the chorus as soon as the school reopened, and put them to work on songs for a spring concert. During class, he was just as tough as he had ever been.

"We have a lot of catching up to do," he said.

The class was smaller, however. Fox Tooth had been sent down south, as his mother had threatened. Evelyn Carbón's parents hadn't wanted her out of school any longer, and had enrolled her in a parochial school. But Sergio was there, and so was Dwaine, although the two no longer hung together.

Augie saw Dwaine at the park more and more, and at school less and less. Dwaine was busier now, closer to the street gang, so he didn't come looking for Augie anymore, and Augie found it easier to stay out of his way.

Sergio never thanked Augie for his help on the day of the concert. Augie never expected it. He noticed, though, that no one at school bothered him now. And although Sergio still called him "Perfessor," Augie kind of liked the nickname.

One afternoon, much to his dismay, Augie found Sergio in the music room, where he had planned to do homework. As Augie stood by the door, uncertain whether he should enter, Mr. Franklin came up behind him.

"I see you've found our fellow scholar," he said.

Sergio grinned and pointed to a desk in the room. "You sit there, Perfessor."

Mr. Franklin frowned. "I am the only person in this room that assigns seating, Mr. Barnaby."

Augie stood still.

"Why don't you take any seat you like," Mr. Franklin said.

Augie stared at Mr. Franklin, then at Sergio. Sergio had his head down, his eyes on a math problem, or so it appeared. Augie walked over toward the desk Sergio had pointed to, then dropped his bag one desk nearer to Sergio. Sergio looked up, caught his eye, and grinned again. Augie grinned back.

Doing homework with Sergio was going to be okay.

One Saturday in early March, Walter drove Augie to Louisa's store.

"I've returned the book, you know," he said.

"Maybe you'll find another one worth reading," Walter said.

Augie thought about that. A book worth reading—that would make the trip worthwhile.

He had just said hello to Louisa when the bells on the front door jingled, and an old white woman walked in. She didn't look as ancient as Mrs. Lorentushki, but Augie thought she did look like someone's grandmother.

"Mother," Louisa said, "I would like you to meet someone."

The older woman turned to Augie. She smiled. Augie noticed how it made the hook in her nose more pronounced. But her eyes shone gray and deep, just like her daughter's. He had the feeling he had seen her somewhere before.

"This is Augie Boretski," Louisa continued. "Augie, this is my mother, Mrs. Nordritch."

A bell went off in Augie's head. Mrs. Nordritch. The one who had married Emmanuel. It couldn't be.

"Pleased to meet you," Mrs. Nordritch said, extending her hand.

Augie shook it. "Nice to meet you, too."

Mrs. Nordritch nodded and took off her jacket. "Louisa has been telling me how she always wanted a godchild."

"Mother!"

Louisa's tone of reproach made both Walter and Augie smile, although Augie tried to hide his smile under a hand.

"Don't mind me," Mrs. Nordritch said. "I just like to cause trouble."

"There is a package waiting for you in the back," Louisa said.

Mrs. Nordritch winked to Augie before leaving them. Louisa shook her head. "Would you like another book?" she asked Augie.

"Well . . . ," he said.

She reached below the counter and brought out a volume.

"This one has a dragon," she said.

Augie read the title: *The Hobbit,* by J.R.R. Tolkien.

"How much will it cost?" he asked. He didn't have much money and didn't want to ask Walter.

"You may borrow it."

He looked at her, unsure. Did she mean it?

"Take good care of it," she added.

She slipped the volume forward, and he lifted it, gently. She had already stopped paying attention to it, asking Walter how he was doing. Augie glanced at the clock on the wall. He had another hour before their return to Camden. He found the black chair at the end of the aisle, sank in, and opened the book. A map with a dragon on it was immediately followed by a drawing of a very little man standing in a large tunnel.

This was going to be good.

When Augie looked up at the white lady and black gentleman in the photo, they stared at him as if they were happy to see him there.

Acknowledgments

In writing this book, I received help and inspiration from many sources. The fairy tale "Donkey Skin" can be found under several names and in a variety of versions. The springboard for my retelling was *Peau d'âne*, written by Charles Perrault in the late seventeenth century. Maria Tatar's *The Annotated Classic Fairy Tales* has a good English translation of the tale. The song "By an' By," written in 1917, is an African American spiritual attributed to Henry Burleigh, an influential gospel singer and composer who wrote between 200 and 300 songs. The song "Light One Candle" was written by Peter Yarrow, and I thank Kathy Gutstein at Alfred

Publishing Co., Inc., for helping me secure permission to use its lyrics. The Big Brothers Big Sisters organization and all its volunteers do a remarkable job, and I thank Shari Adams, who took time to share information about the program with me.

A large number of people have assisted me at every step of the writing process. I want to thank: Doe Boyle, whose keen eye and thoughtful questions were so helpful in the first drafts; Nancy Elizabeth Wallace, who convinced me that fairy tales really do work in the narrative; Jerry Spinelli, who taught me the importance of a boffo first page; Trish Batey, who made me rethink the ending; Meg Greene, for her insights about the vernacular; the Shoreline Arts Alliance, which saw promise in an early draft and named it a finalist for the Tassy Walden Awards for New Voices in Children's Literature; the Shoreline Society of Children's Book Writers and Illustrators, whose members over the years have provided feedback and unending encouragement; and all my friends and family, too numerous to list, who have encouraged and supported me, read drafts, listened to my worries, and put up with my complaints.

Special thanks go to my editor, Lisa Findlay, who found the manuscript in a box and helped me make it the best it could be. Any deficits in the results are all mine.

Last but not least, I thank my children, who were always willing to kibitz when kibitzing was needed, and Jon Bauer, my husband and first reader, who never wavered in his confidence, and without whom this would never have been written.

About the Author

A.C.E. Bauer has been telling stories ever since she could talk (some were real whoppers). After learning how to write, she began handing them out as gifts to her family. Ms. Bauer took a break from writing for a while when she was a lawyer helping poor people, but she couldn't stay away from writing for long. She has returned to fiction and now writes for children of all ages. Born and raised in Montreal, she spends most of the year in Cheshire, Connecticut, and much of the summer on a lake in Quebec. She lives with her husband, two children, and their dog, Speedy.